WORKING STIFF

To Andrei Codrescu -
with pleasure -

WORKING STIFF

a novel

by

John

Richards

1996 : HI JINX PRESS : DAVIS

Acknowledgements:

The author would like to thank Jeff Wine, Sandy Wade and Lee de Avila for their friendship, encouragement and suggestions.

The author and publisher also extend thanks to Jordan Jones, editor of *Bakunin,* in which parts of this novel first appeared.

Printed in the United States of America

Author photograph: Dan Turrett

ISBN 1-57650-098-5
Library of Congress Catalogue Number 96-076624

This is a work of imagination, fiction, with all its exaggerations and lies.

Hi Jinx Press
PO Box 1814
Davis, California 95617

Nothing is funnier than unhappiness, I'll grant you that.

— Beckett

For Rose Marie

There are places in my heart
only you can go

WORKING STIFF

CHAPTER ONE

FATHER'S HANDPRINTS

MOTHER:

He sits there and grinds. I can see by the look on his face there's nothing I can do about it. He starts thinking and the acid drips in his stomach. It's eating holes in it. His cigarette is never out. I think she's going to kill him this time. I tell him to take another pill. It won't hurt, the doctor said, when you need another, take it. Tranquilizers don't hurt. They don't seem to help either, except when he misses one. I see him itchy and fidgety, crawling out of his skin, as he turns things over in his mind. And there's nothing I can do about it. We have to sit this out until she gets back here and gets a job and she'll meet a nice guy and they'll fall in love, get married and that'll be that. All set. Nothing to worry about then. He's tying himself in knots. If I'd known he was like this maybe we'd have skipped children, not had any. He needs a calmer place where nothing happens. He gets so upset by the smallest things and I try to keep everything neat around him and quiet and orderly so they're not coming and going at all hours. But it doesn't work when you have two children.

I told her that he didn't mean it when he calls her lazy and a pig. But I think he does. At least when he's mad, which is all the time, because he never lets anything go. He sits in that chair like the great god Zeus, fuming, big as a volcano. I try to keep things quiet. His stomach keeps churning. He says he can feel it turning over and all that acid washing from side to side and coming up on him and turning his breath sour. He wipes his palms on his pants because they're always pouring sweat and the crease in his forehead keeps getting deeper. He started out with such a smile. When he came up the sidewalk rolling from side to side like a ship and the smile on his face that'd turn to a leer when I wasn't looking, leering at me, and I was embarrassed when I'd catch him at it, but it was for me. He wanted to put his hands on me. I couldn't get enough of him, he couldn't get enough of me, before the children came. Maybe we shouldn't have had children. Nothing turns out the way it's supposed to.

Father:

There's two dribbles off my pecker I should have kept to myself. The girl dribble and the boy dribble. The girl dribble is nothing but trouble and the boy dribble costs me just as much.

If I kept those dribbles to myself I'd have money now. I'd have the house paid off. A bigger house. I'd live in a goddamn mansion with a lawn the size of Briggs stadium. Think I'd have stayed on at Edison for twenty years if I used my hand instead of my wife for those two little dribbles? Once those dribbles were born, they had me, you'd think it's a conspiracy between the bosses and God, to keep working stiffs like me working. They count your children before they pile on the work. "Two kids, hmmm, we can bust his ass this year and next year and the year after, he's not going anywhere. He's gonna do what we say because he's got mouths to feed, count 'em, wide open mouths that if he don't put food in nobody's gonna feed." So they got you. Dribble and pay. That's the law. And any poor son of a bitch doesn't realize it is gonna spend his life swimming up to his balls in some grease pit downriver wondering how the fuck he got there. He's gonna have to put grease in ball joints with a gun shaped like his cock because he didn't know what his cock was getting him into. Dribble and pay. He's got a brood. He's got a nest to feed. Money, money, money. Every time he turns around he's gonna have to shell out hard cash, like peeling the skin off his knuckles every time, because that's what he's got to do to get the money to feed his walking, talking, growing, eating, naked-till-he-covers-them dribbles. And I don't know a working man that came out of World War II whose pecker didn't get him in trouble. Dribble and pay ruined my whole goddamn generation. And I'm no exception.

"When I was single my pockets did jingle.
I wish I was single again."

That's two hard ons I should have packed in ice cubes. I should have slammed my pecker in a car door. Problem is there's no talking to it when it's swinging in the air. You can't ignore it. You can't reason with it. It says, action! Now! It gets a notion one special ass is where it's got to sleep, well, forget it, you're gonna end up with a ball and chain. You keep going back to the same watering hole and you're gonna lose your fortune before you even made it. Dribble and pay. That's the goddamn law and you can count on it more than gravity. There's no getting away from it. Smart thing is use your hand, give a couple of shakes and you're all done. Wag it a couple of times, fan it dry, smile and go have a beefsteak and potato supper. But God help you if you put the wrong dribble in a woman. It's gonna grow up and never go away. You can shove that dribble out the door it'll keep coming back. Like a yo-yo, except the string is tied to your wallet.

I figure those two little dribbles have cost me about three quarters of my income. Which makes it clear I've been laboring under a misconception my whole life long. Like every other man I ever met. This is, we think that thing we got hanging between our legs is for fun, pure fun, whoopee. It's a way you can be in the same room with a woman and you don't have to talk. That's a goddamn miracle in itself. And later the woman can still agree she had a good time. Once in a while. And it *is* for fun. It's God's gift to grown-ups. But there's this little hitch in it. This biology. A misplaced dribble and your ass is slung in a sling for good.

This is the fucking economics of fucking. This house is not the house of my dreams. It's the house I could afford after two kids. And my job is not the job I looked for my entire life. It's the job I have to hang onto with the teeth of a German shepherd so I can hang onto the house I settled for. And where I pay for a lot of food I don't get to eat myself. This is the economics of fucking. And it never ends. You think your kids are going to grow up and go away. But they keep coming back like a case of hemorrhoids.

And some cases are worse than others.

The boy pretty much goes his way and all I have to do is pay.

But the girl busts into blubbery helplessness you'd think she was two years old, and camps out here in my living room. When she gets here I've got to go through all the trouble of getting her out again. I don't think there's a crowbar big enough.

I don't want a lot. I was born a working stiff. I'll die a working stiff. But goddamn it, leave me a little bit for myself. A few crumbs. It's all I ask.

MOTHER:

But I'm glad we did. Because you're not really married until you have children. Then you're a family. You're normal. My mother always said children bring sunshine into your life. That's true. That couldn't be truer. Children make a house glow. I got pregnant when I was still living at my mother's house, we were sleeping on the fold-out in the living room. We've never been alone. And that really gets to him. My mother used to come out into the living room with her coffee and sit on the edge of the bed and start talking before he went to work. So we moved out. We borrowed seventy-five dollars from my father and got a VA loan that got us into our first house. I was showing already. But it was going to be all right because I knew we were going to be a family. Except for those six months, we've never been alone our whole married life. Twenty years there's always been someone else in the house with us. But it was okay when she came along. He'd chase her around the house and she'd squeal and he'd laugh at her and she'd come back around the corner again. I'd see her face sticking around the door of her room wanting him to chase her again. We had the second one. He was his proud son. He used to throw him in the air. "Watch out," I'd say, "You're going to conk that boy on the ceiling." He'd keep throwing him in the air. A boy and a girl. What we wanted, a perfect family. Even though the boy almost killed me coming out. My health broke after that. My nerves were shot. Everything was fine. I had him and was starting to get my strength back and then I started to get nauseous. It didn't go away. It kept up, first mild and then worse. Cramping started in my stomach that kept twisting my insides tighter and tighter like a towel being wrung. In couple of days I couldn't lift my arm. I couldn't even hold my boy on my chest. He'd start to slide over and they'd take him away from me. It was too hard to raise my head. That's what broke my health. The doctor made a mistake when I had him and left some afterbirth inside me. It must have been way up in there where he couldn't see it because he was a good doctor. It was a little piece about the size of a silver dollar, like a little fetus that didn't get flushed out, only it was growing rotten inside me and I think it got a lot bigger like a whole new pregnancy up there, in secret, going all kahooey and putrid that swelled up like a fist and then big as a baby's head and I could feel it up there filling with pus and lumpy with filth from the birth and it must have been covered with bumps like pimples that were bursting in me because that's what it felt like before the doctor figured out what was wrong and went back in there and spooned it out. He scraped and cleaned and washed and he said that would fix me up. But it was too late because of the bursting that was caused by the violence of my vomiting that would crimp me over with convulsions so violent it broke up that lump so it leaked out into me and I had poison then running around in my body, all through my veins that carried it to the ends of my fingers and tips of my hair. My hair lost its shine. I'd feel it pulsing in me sometimes, the poison left by the boy's birth. My skin would get all prickly. I could feel the pores opening up like the poison inside me was inviting the poison outside me to come in. With my skin opened up like that, anything floating in the air could find its way in, be sucked into my skin from there, who knows? to my stomach, my lungs, my brain? It made me afraid to be in the room with someone who sneezed, because you know all those filthy germs shoot out their mouth in a wet cloud and hang there so that even after they sneeze and forget it, the air is still contaminated with filth. With my pores open like that from sickness I could feel the germs settling in the open pores, fester and leak into the inside of me. And that's not all. I was still bleeding for a long time from my female place. More than I should have. It should have healed up and left me alone. But it's like someone pulled a plug under me and I kept draining away. Anytime I was on my feet, the blood would settle and build up pressure and then come running out of me. And with chasing after two kids and then keeping the house clean and bleeding and weak with all the poison that ruined my nerves, I was tired all the time, and I still haven't recovered. Because there's never been any relief. They're always here, the kids, they take cleaning up after or having to be kept in line. Because they're older doesn't make it any less. It's not easy being a mother. But at least we had them. We're a family and we can count on each other. When she gets back here we'll be together again and we can go on from there. I don't mind if they're around because they're our children and at least we can talk to each other. He never talks. Grumpy. Sits there with his nose in a book or a filthy magazine or goes off to the toilet with a crossword puzzle and that's the last I see of him, all Saturday morning, and what do we have the rest of the week but work. Now that the kids are getting older, he wants to close the door and nail it shut. If he had his way, he'd take me off to an island where there's no television, no telephone, maybe a library. And we'd sit. No sounds. No people. No disturbance. Like his father did. Sit on a sun porch somewhere and glare at the seagulls squalling on the sand. The whole earth is supposed to sit quietly out of sight and whisper so he can enjoy himself. Sits there like King Farouk.

But if she's in the house I won't have to worry about her so much. I can keep track of her. It'll be better. She can help me with the housecleaning while she looks for a job and she can help with cooking and dishes. As long as they get along.

FATHER:

"When I got her out of the house was the happiest day of my life. I don't care what she does with herself so she doesn't do it under my roof. I don't want to have to look at it. She wants to wash her face with wet crap she can go right ahead, but don't expect to walk through that door and have me say, 'Oh, honey, oh, so glad you're home.' Bullshit. She can take her lazy ass out that door and find some other poor cocksucker to support her, and believe me, she will, and she'll take that poor asshole for everything he's worth. She's like my sisters and she's like my mother. Take everything she can get. Never met a broad any different. Except your mother. They're all whores."

"Guy, I wish you wouldn't say that."

"Why not? It's the truth, ain't it?"

"How do you think that kind of language makes me feel?"

"Honey, I'm telling you I never met a broad anywhere I could trust except you, and our everlovin' daughter is no exception. She fits right in. You can't trust a word that comes out of her mouth."

"But you make it hard to say anything to you. She's been afraid to say anything ever since she was born."

"Glad Uncle Sam wants her. I've had enough. Maybe the Army can straighten her out. She hasn't got any discipline is the trouble. Never has. You mean to tell me she couldn't keep her room cleaner than a pigsty. When's the last time you saw the top of her vanity fifteen minutes after she strolled in there. Her clothes in a shit-heap in the middle of the floor. It's a wonder she never broke her neck walking to the closet. She's goddamn slob."

"I know honey, but that's no way to talk about your daughter."

"Dad, who cares if her room is a mess."

"I care. As long as *her* room is under *my* roof I care. It's a goddamn fire hazard. It's a wonder her wads of dirty kleenex on the floor, under the bed, on the dresser, piled up around her ashtray didn't burn the place down. It's a wonder we didn't have a goddamn bonfire from her cigarettes. Burn us out of house and home. I get so goddamn mad I could rip her head off, but I figure she'd meet some unsuspecting son of a bitch and marry him and I can wash my hands of the whole mess. I won't say I don't love her, but enough of this bullshit is enough."

"Your father doesn't really feel that way."

"Bullshit."

"Guy, you're saying that. When she was little you played with her all the time on the floor and held her over your head..."

"Dad, why don't you let it go?"

"Because for eighteen years you and your sister have hung on to me like a couple of wet dingleberries. I watched her grow into my sisters and my mother and I'd get sick to my stomach. And now she's finally gone, gone, gone. Hallelujah! I get some peace and quiet and I think all I gotta do is get rid of you."

"Guy!"

"I'm not throwing him out. I'm not throwing you out, boy, but when you get ready to go, let me know, I'll help you pack your bag. I'll wave goodbye from the front porch, you'll see big crocodile tears running down my cheeks. Hardy har har, tears of joy."

"Goddamn it, Guy."

"I love you and your sister. I do. I swear to God. But children are leeches by nature. Can't be any other way. When they're little they can't help it, but goddamn it, when they get a little older, you expect them to be able to leave the nest. And your sister never showed the slightest inclination to get off dead center and do anything on her own initiative."

"You make me so mad. You sit there like the Lord in Judgement."

"Well, excuse my ass, honey, I am Jesus Christ Lord Almighty God in heaven sitting in this goddamn house on a warm, fat turd. And I mean it."

"He doesn't mean it."

"Like hell."

"Your father gets mad at her because she's always leaning on us."

"Every goddamn time that telephone rings costs me money."

"Guy, read your paper. There's nothing wrong with helping

out your daughter. Honey, your father gets tired."

"Tired, my ass."

"Guy, let me talk."

"She's got her hand so deep in my pocket her elbow's bumping my balls."

"He's mad because your sister told us she wants to get out of the Service."

"Can she do that?"

"She wants to come home."

"You make a commitment, you keep it. You sign up for four years, you do four years. You don't whine about it."

"Guy, would you shut up?"

"She crabs, she bitches, she whines. They can keep her. When I went in the Marines, I went. I didn't look back. When a child walks out that door, she's saying 'Piss on the old man, I'm gonna do it on my own.' Well, all right. Let's see you do it. Don't come whining back with her tail between her legs, or for that matter, anybody else's tail between her legs."

"That's enough."

SISTER:

His name is Jack. Jack Jackson. Jack off. Jack around. Hey, Jack. What's doing, Jack? And Jack is strong. Real strong. I told him I didn't want him grabbing me. I'll stay. I'll stay all night. I want to stay, Jack Jackson, I'll jack you off, I said, but don't hold me down. I'll lick the sweat off your neck. I'll lay in your bed and put my skin on your skin. I'll hold you in my fingers and wiggle you till you squirt, but don't hold me down, please don't hold me down anymore. I like these sheets and I like to lay here in my slip next to you and when you put your arm over my shoulder I get wet and your fingers do the job all the way, laying here in the dark with you, you don't have to think of anything, I'll wiggle you till you squirt and then you can sleep and I don't care that you call me stupid and I don't care if you tell me what to do all the time. It's okay, it's okay. If I can lay here. It's a quiet place a long way from home, laying here, and when you're breathing thick from cigarettes and drinking and your skin smells sour from it, I like that, it's sweet to me, you lay here against me and even in your sleep I'll wiggle you,

to make sure I can
to make sure your thing still works
to make sure you still have it for me,

holding you in my fingers and you asleep and wiggling you and feeling you get hard with whiskey on your breath and sour as garbage smell coming out of your skin and you can call me stupid but I can wiggle you hard and you don't even know it cause you're so drunk and sleeping like a fat pig and I can get you squirming and groaning in your sleep and who do you think is stupid with your hard on flagging around and you groaning stupid and your stupid whiskey sleep working hard because my fingers say so, oh, and your hips seesawing like a dog trying to hump my leg in your sleep big stupid Jack off, Jackson, Jack off in the dark garbage man stink man squirter Jack Jack Jack off

"What you doing?"

"Playing."

His eyes are slit open, wicked open.

"Yeah, yeah, yeah. Playing. Mmmmmm. Feel better like this."

"No, Jack, lay still. I almost got you. Lay still. I almost almost almost got you."

"Put your hand away, girl."

I don't like it when he grabs me, shit when he grabs me.

"Pull down these panties, baby, it feel a lot better."

"No."

"Pull 'em."

Big arm and big leg over and between me so I can't move, he makes me still, he grabs me and holds me still so I can't move in a straightjacket coffin of big arms and big legs climbing on top.

"Jack, Jack, stop."

"This way, this the way it's supposed to be."

And is it supposed to feel like he's making a new hole, tearing me open, grunting pig, swearing bitch at me cause he's big all over and holding me down and I can't do anything how he holds me almost feels good but I don't want this, what if he squirts in me, holding my arms over my head and face buried in my hair he's a grunting pig but he holds me and getting bigger in me and I can yell at him but I don't you cocksucker I got you I got you but I don't I can say you big cock belly arms legs I got you breathing with the squirt leaking out your ears and out your mouth and dripping out your fingernails and out your scalp pores makes me laugh big stupid pig squirter fuck machine fuck me Jack Jackson Jacked up Jack hammer Jack rabbit rabbit hips Jack be nimble squirts and then big arms and thick legs and barrel chest and flopping belly and hard shoulders and that hard stick he's so proud that I made stand up like a fat pencil that listens to my fingers falling down folding up becomes mush skin feels like wet lettuce and squirt running down the cheeks of my ass.

"I love you, Jack."

"Yeah, me too."

Who's he love? Him? Me?

"I love you, Jack."

"Yeah, me, too."

fading away rolling off so our skin unsticks and I can move and he falls again in sleep away from me and I bunch his wet lettuce in my hand and tug it with my fingers but he's gone and gone and gone and sour garbage smell comes back and this time I don't like it cause the air is picking the wet off my skin and I can't sleep with him he grabbed me like a piece of shit he owned but at least it's not home and he feels warm and he loves me he said he loves me in a way he loves me.

BROTHER:

She's coming home. I hope she can come home. I want her to be here with me. They beat me, but they didn't beat her. I can talk to her. She's my very own. I love her. They beat me plenty, but she got the worst of it. She was first out the chute.

"Say, look what flopped out, a little girl, well, we'd have a freer hand if it was a little boy, but a little girl, well, let's get to work." They put her on the rack, they started to straighten her out right there in the crib. "Don't drool, don't touch your mouth after you touch your pussy, dirty little thing, dirty little girl."

They started early, glaring at her, long before I was born. When I came along, they were a little bored, they took the easy way out. They slapped me on the ear, they beat the shit out of me, the old lady screamed, of course, she screamed at both of us, threw things, but when it came to hitting, I got it. Slap, spank. She'd flail her arm at me until it was sore, then get the belt to punish me for wearing out her arm. Blistering her hand on my ass. "You little son of a bitch, look what you did to my hand."

But you can believe me, I had it the easiest. When my sister showed up, they were younger, more vigorous. They were ready to really torment her, but were still sentimental, which constrained them enough to keep the attack subtle. They couldn't justify beating the shit out of her because she was their first, and a defenseless little girl at that, so they did it with good judgment, good advice, they did things for her own good. She never knew what hit her. It was all for her own good, wasn't it? Pinching her, scrubbing her clean with towels so rough they could use them to sandpaper a floor. "Got to get you clean, dear," saying what little girls did and didn't do, so she was confused right off the bat. She never got over it either. No question. She got the worst.

When I came along the same techniques didn't work. They glared, I shook, but their patience was gone, and they weren't constrained by sentimentality. After the first time the old lady was torn in two, she knew what it was about, birthing, knew what a filthy, squalling thing you got at the other end of nine months, a greedy mouth, loud, that shit itself without a second thought, puked down her blouse every chance, when I came along she got right to work, slap, whop, I knew the score right away. But she didn't, my sister, she was always wondering, do they love me, do they hate me? Of course they love you, they adore you, but they're parents and don't want love to get in the way of straightening you out. "Get your thumb out of your mouth, you little shit, it's dirty."

I want her to come home. Is that the right thing for her? I don't know, I don't care. I want her to come back to me and talk to me again. With her gone, they've got too much time on their hands to come after me. We were a united front. We could collaborate. When I was little, I had someone to ask, "Are they crazy?" and she said, yes. Thank God she was there to say, yes, something is wrong, out of kilter.

They'll take her back, but they'll make her pay for that room, they'll send her a bill for every minute in front of the bathroom mirror, every cornflake will have a price tag attached, that tag a razor blade that will catch in her teeth and lacerate her tongue.

SISTER:

I have little tits. Jack calls them plums. Calls them golf balls. Calls them Kleenex.

"I noticed there's no Kleenex in the box. You wearing it in your bra? I noticed you're a little bigger today. Gimme a little bit of that," reaching down my blouse, pinching, I'm dancing, try to get away from his big hand. "I need a Kleenex. I gotta blow my nose. You do have *clean* Kleenex down there, don't you? You're not stuffing your bra with Kleenex you picked out of the wastebasket, are you? I don't want to reach down here and come up with snot."

And then he pulls his hand out of my blouse and there's snot on his finger. He must have hid it on his finger all along. "Look at that. She's using dirty Kleenex." Jamie and Bruce bust out laughing at me because he pulled out snot and there's no Kleenex down there.

I got little tits. So shoot me. What good are boobs, anyway? Boob is what you call someone stupid. Hey, boob. Boobs. The stupid twins that hang on the fat lady.

Bruce makes a lunge at Jamie like he's going to check out her tits. She shoves him back down. "You pig," she says at Bruce and says again at Jack. They laugh. And she's laughing. I'm the one that's not laughing because the cause of these high times, big laughs, is my small tits. I wish I had bigger ones. I wish I had heft and size that could swing against my shirt and turn heads like Jamie, who doesn't even bother with a bra a lot of days and wears Bruce's flannel shirt so they swing free inside up against the cloth. Jack's eyes are tied to her tits sometimes by an invisible string. He follows them around the kitchen like they aren't even attached to her, and my eyes are attached to him by a string because I can't take my eyes off him following her tits across the room. Times like this I wish I was home, in my room. With my radio and nothing else.

Mom said, "You'll fill out. There's full women in the family, both grandmas." But big boobs slipped by her. She's little as me. She said it'd come to me, though, like diabetes, she said, every other generation gets tits, I'd get big and men would get bug eyed when I walk, and so I waited for them to grow, to plump up from little stones that poked out. I touched them and bunched them in my fingers and tried to push out my chest when I looked sideways in the mirror. I pulled in my breath, panted shallow to try to keep my tits far out away so they looked big, but mother sighed and father called them buttons. My blouse hung in the front, an empty sack, no potatoes to fill it. I'm not big. Jack seems to like me anyway. He pulls me on top of him on the couch, but his eyes stay tied to Jamie when she walks through the living room, and I haven't got the tits to put in his face to erase her from his eyes.

Mother said, "Don't let anyone touch you here. Men are dirty things that'll want to take off your shirt and take down your pants. Don't let them touch you." She was saying this before she realized that when they peeled back my blouse they'd find nothing there. Little stones. Little plums. Some men have bigger tits than me. I don't think it matters. They still come after me. Maybe that's why it's called a piece of ass and not a piece of tit. And still they're not so small. They're the size of my fists and they're shaped nice.

Jack nuzzles me and he hasn't busted his nose on my breastbone. They bulge a little on the bottom so the nipples lift, and he licks that, runs his fingers along the side of them. They're not too small to feel good when he does that. He notices them a lot, running his finger over the silk skin and down my side. He starts me shivering with a touch. But if my tits were bigger and filled his whole hand, if they were heavy and soft I could wrap them around his head. His eyes would never stray. Then he'd never leave me. If they were warm, soft pillows and flowed milk on his tongue he'd never leave me. But I'm little. A snack he'll take and move on. I know he's going to move on.

Goddamn Jamie and her tits.

FATHER:

"I joined the Marines when I was seventeen years old and my pappy had to sign for me. I told him I wanted to join he didn't say a word, got back up off his chair, went to the kitchen cupboard and pulled down two water glasses. He poured about that much whiskey in one and about that much whiskey in the other one and said, 'Drink up, boy.' It hit bottom so hard it burned the soles of my feet. Then he picked up his hat and shoved out the screen door with me towing behind.

"When I told my mother, she beat her breast, walked room to room lamenting the lost soul her poor baby boy, like they took me out feet first. 'I lost my baby, I lost my baby, how can you do this to me?' To her? What the hell did I do to her? 'My baby, my baby.' The faucet turned on and she had two steady streams running out of her eyes and dripping off her chin. 'How could you do this to me?'

My pappy filled up another glass and sat out on the back porch sipping whiskey all night, and when I went out there, I must have had a scared shit look on my face because he said, 'Boy, don't you ever repeat this I'm saying, but I'm saying ignore what she's saying. There's one thing a woman's good for.'

"What's that?

"'You'll find out presently. They're good for one thing, and then one of them gives you children so you stay with her. I went in when I was fifteen, I got shot in the hip. I got mustard gassed. I saw my friends chewed up on the ground and I did what I had to do. But when I walked out from behind my mother's skirt I grew up and I didn't look back. You ignore her and go pour yourself another shot and come out here and sit with me.' My mother was crying and all my sisters were in there with their arms around her and I sat there with my father until two in the morning and he didn't say another word.

"And I went out of that house and I didn't look back. I didn't ask another thing. And I didn't take another thing. I washed my hands of them and they washed their hands of me. I don't get this with your sister. She says, 'Okay, piss on you, I'm going in the Service,' and then she keeps running back to the well. Let me tell you: This well is running dry. What am I supposed to do, carry her on my back for the next thirty years? This is eating holes in my stomach. I get so goddamn tense my jaw aches. She's putting me in an early grave. She's bleeding me until I got sand running out my veins. She needs a car, okay, we send her money for a car. But she can't get a decent car, she gets a pile of rust drops the transmission next day. Phone rings. 'Oh, daddy, daddy, daddy.' I send her more money. It's a good car. Sure. Phone rings. Tires are bald tubes. She didn't notice they were bald, what's she blind? I'm not going to let her kill herself on them so I send her more money. She's so lonely. She's got to come home for President's Day. President's Day? What kind of holiday is that? She can't stand it, gotta come home. Your mother starts working on me. More money. I don't begrudge a little help, but Jesus Christ, I'm not the Federal Reserve Bank. She thinks I print it in the back room. What do you need, honey? Two hundred, four hundred, a thousand! Now you're talking, why mess around? A thousand, you bet, right away. I'm working so she has every little thing her heart desires. So she can smile and be happy and run around without a care in the world. I'd say that's a good reason for me drag my ass out of bed every morning, so I can keep the tears off her cheeks. See her happy smiling face.

"Now she's not content to bleed me through the telephone. She's chasing home so she can sit in the back room and send out her requests on a silver platter. Home is the unending gravy train, her personal treasury, and me and your mother are her personal handservants put on God's earth to do her bidding, wait on her hand and foot. When is this going to stop? Someone's got to call a halt. See that. I'm putting up my hand and stopping the train. The gate came down. She can run all over Hell's Half Acre doing whatever she's doing out there, but for Christ's sake, let her do it out there.

"Believe me, honey, our everlovin' daughter isn't going to girl scout meetings, she's not going to tea parties. She's on an Army base, maybe two hundred women surrounded by thirty thousand men. You think she's sitting around watching *Donna Reed* with thirty thousand stiff peckers on the parade ground?"

"Guy, she's nineteen years old. She's not thinking about sex all the time with a filthy mind like you."

"Honey, I was nineteen years old in the Service once and that's the only kind of minds they got. And what the hell else do you think of when you're nineteen? I went in a fresh spanked babe in arms, like our little angel, and real fast I grew a little red halo with horns on it. And baby, ain't you glad?"

"Can't you think of anything else?"

"Dad, she doesn't act like that."

"Here's the expert."

"Guy, you know she doesn't act that way."

"No, I don't know that. And I don't care. I'm not losing sleep over it."

"Well, she doesn't."

"Okay, I'm convinced. You say she doesn't, honey, and she doesn't."

"And she's going to come home and I don't want to hear any of this when she's back. We're going to take care of her."

BROTHER:

He's sitting there in the front room reading with this look on his face, and she's clicking the nail polish off her thumb, click, wait a bit, click again, wait, click, working her nails clean, click, and I'm a shadow in the hallway, deep hidden, still, watching. We're frozen waiting for her to come home. He swings his leg over the arm of the chair and turns the page. When she looks up from her nails, it's only to look at the carpet in front of her chair. Did somebody do something wrong? Nobody did anything yet. We're waiting for her to get here, and then what? She's home. We've always been waiting for this, or something, her clicking her nails a sharp sound like a dentist's tool working under the gums and I can't breathe in and I can't breathe out and I can't breathe deep and I can't breathe shallow and she can't breathe sitting there with the afghan over her lap and clicking off the nail polish. The lights are yellow. The whole room has the look of dirty yellow teeth, smoked on teeth, like his teeth that turned yellow with the smoke he keeps churning out, crooked yellow murky teeth, this room as crooked and yellow and murky coated in the chimney filth he keeps churning out. I don't want to move. I don't want to walk through the front room where they sit because it's something I'm doing wrong if I disturb the yellow light, make the smoke push this way or that. I'm *supposed* to be a shadow in the hallway. The phone doesn't ring. There are no relatives or neighbors stopping by. This is ours. Our long moment. The moment that's been going on since I can remember.

She says, "Don't tell the neighbors."

Tell them what? That she's coming home? What neighbors would I tell? Why would they care? Saying, "We don't want you to go blabbing around to all the neighbors and telling them all the things that are going on around here."

What's going on? Nothing. She's clicking. He's flipping the

pages with that look on his face like he's eating something bad. He reaches up and picks a spot of tobacco off his tongue and wipes his finger on his dungarees, without looking up, without looking at her or me. How can a minute last so long? How can your heart beat and beat and beat when you don't breathe? Tell the neighbors what? That there's nothing going on in this house, nothing at all, we're statues, we're frozen sitting in this house and nothing happens, we're a tomb you can walk into year after year and nothing happens, it's quiet, he's reading with that look on his face and she's clicking and I'm shadow, darkness, draped against the wall. I wouldn't know what to tell the neighbors. Should I knock on the neighbor's door and say, "So you know, there's nothing going on at our house. I hope that sets your mind at ease. The orgies I know you and your husband imagine taking place, they're not taking place. My mother doesn't run through the house naked chased by my father in a loincloth. We're not dissecting stray dogs. Or lost children. We don't violate statues of the Virgin Mary. We don't even eat with our mouths open. We use the bathroom one at a time. And my father hasn't once fallen down the stairs because my mother got drunker than him and pushed. My mother figures you and your husband and your beady eyed brats have been lurking at our window sill trying to glimpse the wild goings on over here. Your listening devices have proven insufficient to amplify and uncover the corruption in our house. So I'm here to tell you, so you know, so you can put your minds at rest: Nothing is going on over there in my house. Nothing!"

Really nothing.

We're waiting for her to come home.

Before that we were waiting for her to go.

Before that we were waiting for her high school to end.

Before that we were waiting to see how she did in high school.

And we waited for other things, too.

We waited for my father's father to die.

And we waited for my great-grandmother to die.

We waited for my mother to finish beauty school.

And my sister to finish charm school.

We waited for my grandmother to die.

We waited.

We waited for runny noses to stop and coughs to subside.

And then we waited, expectantly, with our breath held (maybe that's where the habit of not breathing came from), for our noses to run and coughs to start again.

We waited for the fall, and then the winter. We waited for the tomatoes to bear fruit and the winter to put an end to it.

We waited for the results of the blood test.

The lung x-ray.

We waited until the car was paid off.

So we could buy another car because when that one was paid off we could buy another and we have to wait and we can buy another one.

Because if we wait, everything will be taken care of at last, the house will be paid for, and there'll be enough money in the bank and our illnesses will finally be cured and there will be no more anything coming down on us when we least expect it, and we'll be through school, done with work, cleanly, clearly, crisply in control, at last, if we can be patient and wait for everything to get in order. Because it will if we do the right thing, which is wait, quietly, wait, him in that chair, her clicking her nails, me watching from the hallway, *in* the room with my eyes, but *out* of the room with all the rest of me, waiting right now for her to get home, because when she does then that major thing will be done in our lives, the awfulness of separation when she went out there away from us into the world where "anything can happen." Yes, I know, mother, anything *can* happen, and it does, unless we stay still, the pages of his magazine turning with a sharp startling sound and I see the yellow flesh-colored stain of those naked women page after page, smudged by the smoke, and the smudge of the women coming off on his fingers like nicotine.

SISTER:

"I'm telling you, I don't want to go home. It's the last place on earth I want to go. When I left home it was the happiest day of my life. I cried all the way to Basic, but that's because I was scared about what I was getting into, not because I was sorry to leave home. You don't know what it's like. I don't know where else to go. I've got to get out of the Army. I can't stand it. All the stupid things. So I've got to go home for a little while. Until I get some money together. You don't know what it's like. Let me tell you, my room, they're crazy about my room. It's *my* room. It's full of *my* things. I want *my* things *my* way. They don't. They pick on things. My mother likes to clean. She's white glove all the way. When we were little, me and my brother had to clean the house with her. You should have seen the way she swings a dust mop. Babe Ruth, Sultan of Mop. Wham, against the floorboards, then she'd send us off to our rooms with it and look under the bed and if there was one speck of dust under there, she'd come after us. You think she could chase dust balls, you should have seen her chase us down. Whop, whop. She could use a mop for more than dust balls. You should have heard my brother yell, he was good at running, but she always caught him. Then she'd go over the blinds with her finger, see if we got every slat. Try that when you're eight years old, see if you know an eight year old that can get every slat. They were always bugging me about my room."

"For all that, you still turned out to be a slob."

"So."

"Nothing. It's all right. Who cares?"

BROTHER:

The old man's complaining about his stomach. Bad sign. He pushes his hand into his stomach as if he's trying to push back a wild beast that's gnawing through. There's no ulcer, he's been checked for that, so maybe he actually does have a wild beast trying to get out. He's pushing it back because the easiest exit isn't out his belly, it's out his mouth. Every time he pushes back, his head rears and the beast roars. "Goddamn, the two of them are bleeding me dry."

The old lady is dusting, cleaning ashtrays. The dishes in the cupboard are so clean they squeak when nobody even touches them.

I want her to come back.

The phone rings. A collect call.

"Goddamn it." The beast in the living room.

She talks to her, whispering, then, "Yes, sweetheart. That's all right. Yes. But did you find out the *kind* of discharge you're getting. Yes, I know you only want to get out, but your father says you should try to get an honorable one."

"I don't give a shit what she gets."

"I know, honey. We want you to come home, too. We'll send you a ticket."

"Goddamn it."

"Guy."

They talk some more and then it's my turn.

"Mark?" Her voice is thin and high like it's squeezing through a narrow tube. "They're letting me out. I'm coming home." Then she's crying, a wet sound like water chugging out a hose. When I said goodbye to her at the airport, she kissed me on the lips and her mouth was so soft and spongy and wet I almost jumped back. Now this chugging.

"That's good. I'm glad." I'm choking, too. My own water pump kicking in.

"It's awful here."

"I know it."

"It's stupid."

"I know."

"I want to come home."

"Come home."

The chugging deeper now, settling in.

"Dad said you did things there."

"What things?"

"With guys."

"I didn't."

"I know you didn't."

"I wouldn't. Do you believe me?"

"Yes."

"Do you *believe* me?"

"Yes."

"Mark, that's disgusting. I didn't do anything. Jack wants me to, but I won't. I can't. Not until I'm married."

"You stay at his place."

"Of course, I do. Women's barracks are awful. You can't even pee without them listening to you. They're all bitches. And dykes. But when I stay with Jack I don't do anything. I don't. But I can't stay in the barracks."

SISTER:

I won't tell him. I can hear in his voice he wants me to say no, no I don't do anything with guys, I don't let them touch me, and I never let them do it to me. That's what he wants to hear. That's what I have to tell him. What would happen to him if I told him that Jack holds me down and does it to me, and that I don't want him to, but he does. He lays me open like a shirt, he unbuttons me from the chin all the way down and fits inside me. When I try to push him away he pulls at the cloth, he rips me open, I can't hold him back, Mark doesn't know what it's like to be opened up like that, I try to not do it with Jack, but he pushes back the edges and opens me up, and climbs on top of me with all his weight so I can't move and he says that I have to, I have to move and that gives him pleasure.

"No, I don't let him do anything. That's disgusting. How could you think that? Never. I won't let anybody do anything to me."

He believes me. He's the only one that believes me so I have to tell him that nothing happens. Though I don't always have to be held down. There are times Jack doesn't hold me down and I even get on top of him and it's okay, and it's like I unbutton myself and fit around him, a blanket, a shirt that fits right against his skin and though I don't have much on my chest, he strokes me there and slides in me slow so good, nobody can know about it, how it feels, I don't even let Jack know, and I can't tell Mark because his voice is so small when he asks and he doesn't want me to, so I can't tell him I do, I can't tell him that sometimes when Jack is on top of me, or throwing me over on my face and lifting me up and doing me that I think I'm one of those girls in Dad's magazines, that I'm big tits and wide ass that Jack wants that he can't have with me, that he really wants but he has to settle for me, small waisted and small assed and small tits, but I'm for a little while wide open and filthy as he wants, gaudy perfume and pink lipstick and pink lips curled around his stick. Like those girls in those magazines, I lay there with my legs split and my eyes looking in his eyes so when he does me he can see I see him doing me, or sometimes, like those girls in my father's magazines that he used to hide in the basement by his workbench, where I should not have been when I was too young, where I shouldn't have seen, I didn't understand, I offer myself backwards, like a dog, up on my knees, but with my face in the pillow looking back at him, watching him climb around. Jack monkey dick Jack.

I made him say he believed me thinking that when he said it, I know him, when he said it, if he said it, then he had to believe me or he couldn't have said it at all. So I know he believes that I don't do anything.

"That's disgusting," I said and when I said it I could feel how disgusting it is and I felt Jack's handprints now all over me, I was covered with handprints, I felt like one of my father's magazines and my father was holding it in his hands and looking down at me there with my legs split and white dribble down my thighs from doing it with Jack and my father saying, "That's disgusting. You're a whore and a slut and I wouldn't piss on you without thinking that I'll catch something," rattling the pages with me on them, and then wrinkling and crumpling them in his hands so Jack's hands leave dirty handprints on me from the magazine print, from the sweat his hands give off when he's doing me.

And I want to be away from where he is so he can't split me and hold me down and make me this way. That's why I have to go home to my room, where no man can put his handprints on me in my room. I'll be alone and can shut the door and listen to the radio, me and the radio.

Brother:

Naturally, my sister can't return to a filthy house. We've got to get it cleaned up. After all, this is homecoming. We've got to do it right. She lived here her whole life and we can't have her surprised by the heaps of dirt spilling out from under the beds, the closets awash with dustballs the size of tumbleweeds, you could break your toe. The living room rug has so much lint you'd think a mattress was shredded in there. The window sills! God, the window sills have layers of dust thick as a finger! You could curl up under that blanket of dust and go to sleep. You'd be warm as a down comforter. And the cobwebs! When did all those spiders crawl in here, spinning their nasty tents, gluing them to the corners way up where you've got to bat them with a broom and even then who knows what goo remains snatching specks of dust from the air and attaching them to the wall. That's how streaks begin. Subtle, invisible attachments of dust, accumulations of dirt that hang like shit from the ass end of a goldfish and lay across the wall, staining. Get it now before it's permanent. Get the house in order. Quick! Quick! We've got a lot to do. Clean out the cupboards, the dirt carried there on the filthy feet of insects so small you can't even see them (or we'd have crushed them with our thumbs). The dirt. The filth. It's got to go.

The old lady's got her implements out. She's throwing brooms, dustpans, mops, sponges, buckets, the vacuum cleaner, Spic and Span, dish soap, Lava, detergents of all kinds, not to mention rags, feather dusters, spray polish and deodorants out of the broom closet. She's pulling jars, jugs, powders, steel wool and rubber gloves from under the sink. She's setting the house in motion. I sling kitchen chairs into the living room. The wastebasket, stools. Roll out the hairdryer. Slopping buckets of suds over the linoleum, then down on my knees, scrubbing out skids. The old man is grunting in the front room, shoving the davenport away from the wall.

Amazing the crap we've kicked under the couch in the week since the last time we moved everything. Ten pieces of lint! One as large as a hangnail! The vacuum cleaner bumps over the old man's foot as my mother pursues a stray hair.

"Jesus!"

"Watch out!"

No quarter is given. We've got to scour the foulness from corners, impurities from the kitchen drain. She tells me the nauseating truth about the leaks in the house, how the abominable air comes swooping under the door, through the cracks in the windows, between the rafters in the attic spewing slime and grime tainted with nauseating fungus that invades the fabric of our Lazy Boy. Upholstery is a tiny screen that filters smutty, reeking, squalid obscenities too fine for our sweat blurred eyes to detect, keeps them trapped.

Every time we touch the arm of a chair untold billions of maggoty microscopic bacteria burrow in the grooves of our fingerprints. My sister had the right idea at seven years old when she refused to touch doorknobs, and kept indoors, away from the dirty dirt that's everywhere down to the core of the earth. Better to stay in her bedroom inside a plastic bag.

I hear beds slam walls, night tables scrape across the hardwood. The dust mop clicks past. I'm pulling down the light fixtures, vacuuming the clumps of crud out of the heater vents.

She's coming home. She's coming home.

What better excuse for a cleaning party.

The old lady's polishing picture frames.

The old man is waxing under the basement stairs.

The old lady is running a toothpick along the toe molding, getting in the corners.

The old man is dusting the shower curtain hooks.

The old lady is on the lawn with a butterfly net, catching soot before it lands on the roof.

I do what I'm told to do. I'm no fool.

Faster. You missed a spot. A speck. A dot. A particle. My arm aches all the way up to my neck. I beat and pound, rub, scrub, wring and hose. I'm trying to split atoms of filth to banish it once, at last, finally and for all time, to create a clean universe. So the old lady can rest. What else? What could be more fulfilling than seeing her beatific repose, satisfied for a few moments that the world here, in this house, is purged. The air as clean as the breath of an old-fashioned virgin. Metal bright as a new penny. Vases shiny as cat's eyes. Tabletops reflecting her happy face.

SISTER:

Sleepy Jack, Jack off, Jackson. I'll put my clothes on now and you'll never see me naked again. Sleep, Jack, sleep. Breathe deep, breathe soft. I'll forget you. I'll forget your tongue and your thumbs, I'll forget your thighs, your sighs, I'll erase you clean away. I'll turn you into a ghost, Jack, Jack off, Jackson. You can stand in my garden and tap at the window, but I'll never open it, I'll never even pull back the curtains, you'll never see me naked again, Jack, Jack off, Jackson. You can whine like a shivering dog and rip your hair bare and beat hard knuckles against the walls and roof for all I care, but I'll never never ever let you in again. I'm going to step out of the shadows of this room and wash away the filth. I'm going to dream myself clean. I'll forget I ever touched you or what you look like or what you taste like or the smell of your sperm on my fingers. I'll heal my virgin skin, be pure and blessed. Forget you. I won't remember the first time you stroked my wrist or the last time you shoved into me. I won't remember the color of your hair or the food on your tongue when you laughed. It's all a mistake. Everything I've done is a mistake. I'm going to start over fresh, like flowers, like butterflies, a new day that doesn't remember any other day, leaves the dark night behind, shines bright and crisp and clean and doesn't want anything from anywhere, just shine, shine, shine.

I'm going to burn my uniforms and my shoes and I'll burn my memory of you and remember this, Jack, Jack off, Jackson, you're the only one that will ever touch me, ever touched me, and when I forget your face and your name and your eyes, then no one will ever have touched me at all. Nothing will have ever been inside me, I'll be a little girl again, a white communion dress. So sleep, Jack, Jack off, Jackson, and get invisible right before my eyes.

"You going now?"

"Yeah, I want a early start."

"Have some coffee."

"No, I want to get going."

"I'll make it."

What must have woke him, the suitcase scraping the floor. Getting out of bed, slow, looks like he's got disease. But his underpants don't have disease.

"Mr Pecker says, 'Good morning, honey.'"

It makes me laugh. His body gives off under-the-covers heat when he walks over and leans against me. A sleepy smell that makes me want to sleep. He never made coffee for me before so I put down the suitcase. My other wrist is breaking from the weight of the clothes hangers. He takes them out of my hand and lays them on the chair and starts fitting himself against me.

"Coffee, Jack."

"In a bit. Time for play."

"There's no time."

My voice sounds hollow in my head. His fingers tighten on my hair.

"There's time. There's always time."

He bends my head back to get at my mouth. It starts to hurt. My mouth is tired of his mouth. The morning smell of his breath spreads a sewer over my teeth. He's fit up against me so I can feel him urgent and bumping me, a little hint he's giving me while he kisses, like "Get it? Get it? Know why I'm bumping? Get it? Get it?" and he pushes his chest up against me, swelling it barrel big and rubbing back and forth against my chest like saying, "See how big I am, how big and strong, what woman could resist?" He takes my hand and lays it along the shaft of his thing and gets a hitch in his breath and I think how he'd feel if I wrapped my hand around his thing and tugged, and then tugged harder and then harder and lifted him off the floor and swung him around over my head, stretching his thing out like a lasso, banging his head against walls and yelling, "Yahoo!!"

That's that. It's all over.

"What the fuck you laughing about?"

I say, "Nothing," and try to pull him close to me again to cover the laughing.

"What the fuck is so funny?"

"Nothing," and I try to straighten down my face with my hand like straightening a wrinkled shirt and that makes me laugh, too, worst kind of laugh, when something really gets me, with a little snort at the end of the laugh, snort, laugh, snort.

"You sound like a donkey. And I don't want goddamn coffee."

"But, honey, it's good to the last drip," thinking about the spills and drips from his thing and stretching it out like a rope. It's too much.

He's turned his back on me now, and suddenly I want him to do me, I want him to want me again, for it all not to end, and I'm tugging on his arm, trying to pull him to the bed, but he doesn't want the laughing me, doesn't want anything to do with the me that laughs. He stays turned away from me.

And before I know it, I'm on the road.

Father:

"I don't know why in hell she's got to come back here. If I was young, I'd keep going. To where the sun does shine. There's nothing in this town. It's dying. The factories are spilling assholes in the street faster than sewage. Drive down Gratiot Avenue and count the plywood windows. They're burning down the guts of the city. What's left in Detroit? Blacks and rats and pigeons. She's coming back *here*? What does she think she's going to find? Go and keep right on going. That's my motto. Once this place was thriving. When I got out of the war, there was work. People coming up from the South, families starting out here. Jobs everywhere. They were begging for workers. Couldn't get enough of us. We had a strong union so you didn't have to shit every time a boss looked at you. That was protection. They didn't like it, you could file a grievance and make it stick. Right up their asses. They didn't like that. They busted heads out there on the Rouge, but they lost."

"This is her home. She lives here. This is where she belongs."

"You belong where you can make a living and don't forget it. What's she gonna end up with here? A factory rat and fat belly. Half a dozen mouths to feed and nothing but lint to put in them."

"She'll have us. She'll have family."

"Family doesn't count shit if you don't eat. You can't eat grass. You can't eat trees. Hell, there's no trees left to eat. The bugs already got them. Remember the elms when we moved in. It's a sign. Rotten and gone. The city's eaten alive. My pappy grew up on a pig farm south of the Mason-Dixon. My grandfather was a drunk run over by a train when my old man was fourteen years old. Right after the boys kicked his ass and threw him out for beating up my grandma. That farm was the homeplace. My grandma sold quilts and rabbits to feed them and keep them on it. But when the time came to lift their heads up and decide what they were going to do in this life, each one of them put on his hat, spit in the flowers in front of the porch and walked away. Go where there's something to go to. They came to Detroit. Back then it made sense. Much as they loved the old lady, much as they wanted to keep the farm, they walked away from it because it was a loser. What do you see in this town? You see these kids chopping down telephone poles because they've got nothing better to do. Only thing they can sell downtown is steel gates you pull over the plate glass. There's a bar on Gratiot with a sign in the window says, IF YOU CAN'T STOP, SMILE AS YOU GO BY, well, if she had any sense, she'd smile and keep on going."

"Well, she's not. She's coming home."

"Then she's a goddamn fool."

"Dad, maybe she isn't strong enough to keep going right now."

"Who's strong enough? You think I'm strong enough? I got weak lungs that keep folding up on me. What have I had, three, four collapsed lungs. Puts you right down on the deck. Just like that."

"Doesn't stop you from smoking."

"No, and it's not going to. I'll go to hell in a basket of my own device. And my blood's polluted so bad it almost killed me. Remember? And my ass is tired. And I'm pissed off. But I keep going. Strong, who's strong? You got a choice: Keep going or shrivel up like a dry leaf, crumble and blow away. Most of us keep going. And she's not any weaker and she's not any stronger than the rest of us. When you come from where we come from, you pick up a wrench or a broom or a spatula or a hammer and you go to work. You don't think about it. You don't question it. That's what you were born and bred for. To work. And you're going to have to work for cocksuckers because that's the only kind that become bosses. If they had any balls, they'd pick up a shovel with the rest of us and do their part. So you get used to it. You eat ashes. You eat shit. You eat shit till it's coming out your ears. You eat shit because that's what they're feeding you this week and next week. And the week after that won't be any better."

"Jesus, there's more to life than that."

"Yeah? You tell me what it is. You looking for a flower garden. You think this is Eden, boy, you're looking at the wrong map. This is Detroit. Any flowers you find here got teeth. Chew your ass you sit on them. The last time an angel landed in the backyard, they hit him over the head and stole his wallet. He's stumbling around the alley like he's drunk and the rats bit holes in his wings. My boy, that is *your* guardian angel. Take a good look and you know how much you can count on him. Which is to say, you got to work. And your sister's got to work. And your mother. And me. And we're doing nothing more glorious than hauling rocks like slaves in "The Ten Commandments." I don't care what name they put on it. It's nothing more glorious, and it's not any easier and it's not any less inevitable, and the sooner you and your sister get that through your thick heads the better off you'll be."

"She knows she's got to work."

"Where, for Christ's sake?"

"She'll find a job."

"For working stiffs like us there's nothing worse than not having stones to haul. When they run out of stones, the bosses live off the fat. Me and you, we're supposed to eat the sidewalk. You want to know why there's neighborhoods around here you can't walk down the street. Because they tried the sidewalk and it didn't taste so good. So the only thing left to eat is each other. That's what happens when they run out of stones for us to haul, fuck-ups become cannibals, and the rest of us lose our asses."

"You got a job."

"One of the few."

"And don't tell me it's that bad. If it's so bad, why don't you quit."

"Because I'd have to find the same thing somewhere else. I spent my years as a monkey dick climbing up and down electric poles. Great in the summer, you're outside, sunshine, you're your own boss for the most part. But in January, you can hear your balls clinking together. And I'm not about to start over. I work inside now. I got more assholes to contend with every day, but I haven't got the icicles growing off my pecker. And I don't care what job it is, when you start you're at the bottom of the ladder doing something nobody else wants to do."

"Okay, so she'll find a job here."

"That's what I'm telling you meathead, there's no fucking jobs. Stand out on Eight Mile Road and you'll get run over by companies folding up tent and hauling ass out of here. They can't give away the fucking cars they're making. And anything left behind gets incinerated. Look at Twelfth Street. Burned blocks right to the ground. And you know what? Nobody gives a shit!"

SISTER:

I'm home.

FATHER:

Whoopee.

MOTHER:

God, I'm so glad you're here. We love you. When's the last time you washed your hair?

CHAPTER

TWO

I

WAS

LUCKY

SISTER:

The door to my room opens as I'm drifting off to sleep. Two officers are standing over me, glaring down, the one tapping his nightstick against his palm. The other one says, "C'mon, you're going back to the base."

"No, I can't, I can't," I say, a knot rising in my throat.

"You're goddamn right going back. Into the laboratory. We need a urine sample. And some blood. We didn't get you right the first time."

He turns to the officer with the stick and says, "See to it."

I can't go back. I can't go back.

In the Army everybody is always giving you orders. They're telling you what to do and they don't like you no matter how much you try. The officer flicks the stick, clipping my knuckles where I clutch the covers. I jerk back my hands. He hooks the blanket and flips it open. I thought I was wearing a nightgown, I thought I was covered like I'm supposed to be, like I should be, but I'm bare naked and the one officer with an I-Knew-It smirk on his face looks at the other one and they both smirk down at me. I'm streaked with mud and try to cover my breasts but can't, because I'm not alone, it's not only me under the covers, but Jack there, sound asleep, I can't move him off me, he's not asleep, not asleep after all, but dead, and stiff as a tree trunk. But what's more is he has two fingers stuffed up me, and I'm stuck there, pinned down like a dissection, can't move.

I open my eyes and stare at the room half-lit from the alley and realize Dad has gotten up to go to the bathroom and woke me. I forgot. I forgot how he gets up in the middle of the night every night and how I've always heard him, pissing loud enough to drown every dream in the house.

Awake again.

In this house.

Couldn't sleep with Jack, always awake, looking at him in bed next to me, and now alone, in the house again, without Jack, without anybody, listening to the piss run out of my father, thumping the water in the toilet bowl.

Because I didn't know where else to go.

And even the first day, the first minute back:

"You shouldn't have driven all that way by yourself. What if something happened."

"Nothing happened."

"You drove in that shitheap!"

"Where's the bag we gave you when you left?"

"It got stolen."

"Jesus."

"You mean you turned your back on it, without a thought in your head, and somebody strolled up and took it. It figures. Why don't you watch your things?"

"When I was signing out, the NCO told me to leave my bags against this wall, and when I got back it was gone."

"Why'd you leave it?"

"He told me to. He's an officer."

"Is this something new? You do everything any one tells you to? Wish you could do a little bit of that around here."

"What was I supposed to do?"

"Is this how you're going to keep your hair?"

"No, they made me keep it short."

"It looks nice short."

"I want to grow it longer."

"Needs washing."

"Mother, I've been driving half the damn night. Since four a.m.!"

"Don't swear at your mother."

"I'm sorry. I didn't take time to shower."

"I don't know how you can stand it."

"I can't stand it. I can't stand it."

"Me, neither."

"Who could?"

"Honey, what are you so upset about?"

"Nothing."

"We're so glad you're home. Go take a shower."

She gave me a hug and it felt good, even with that little sniff when she put her head next to mine. I wasn't that bad. I couldn't have smelled that bad, could I? I have to get clean. Start over. She smelled the awfulness. I have to wash right away.

After that we talked for a couple of hours and waited for Mark to get home.

Dad's going back to bed and I can hear the hurt of the springs as he settles in, then buzzing and scraping like someone digging in the wall, but it's only the two of them muttering to each other. So she's awake. And he's awake. And I'm awake. And probably Mark's awake, too, upstairs. All of us awake in the night looking into our dark rooms, lit by alley light. A car passing down the street going where in the night? Anywhere in the night, not to be looking into the dark half light of our rooms. Some man passing down the street looking for a woman and I scoot lower in the covers so he won't find me.

Talked for hours before Mark got home.

"I don't want to be a lab tech anymore."

"After the money we spent to send you to that fucking school."

"I don't want to look at another urine specimen. I don't want to listen to another cruddy doctor tell me how to do my job when I know better than he does."

"He's the doctor, but you know better."

"Doctors don't know everything."

"Your problem is you know too much."

"Maybe I can get you in at my place. There's always openings in the typing pool. Too bad you didn't take that steno course."

"I don't want to be a steno."

"What are you going to do, sit on your ass?"

"Should I sit on my head, would that be better?"

"You're already sitting on your head."

"I'll get a job."

"It seems like you don't want to do anything."

For hours.

Then Mark came home and I put my arms around him and started to cry. Mom stood up like she wanted to put her arms around us, too, but she didn't. She circled us and Mark and I held tighter. He's been here all along, in this house.

I didn't have anywhere else to go.

Another car passing down the street, another man looking.

Hey, mister, I'm over here. I'm over here.

BROTHER:

I walk in the door and nobody even knows I'm late. I'm full up with excuses, without any use for them. The part that was going to convince them, how I had to help Father Carey, fag father of our parish, haul out bags of leaves from behind the rectory. "I was on my way home when Father Carey..." Whoops, stop right there. She's home and they're not even listening to me. She's home. I can feel trembling start down in my legs, like water shuddering through the pipes. She stands there with her arms out. And I have the best excuses for being late.

"Father Carey at the parish . . . hauling those bags . . . started to wonder about my spiritual well-being, he was musing, I had to sit there and talk to him. It was good for me. I think I got a lot out of it. I'm going to go back and talk to him again."

I won't tell them a few years ago, before mass, when I was an altar boy, preparing to serve Mass, pulling on my robe, he put his arm around me, squeezed his belly against me, and called me, "Honey." Then they'd know there's not a chance I'd let Father Weirdo talk to me, get me behind the rectory. Talk? Some talk if he ever got me back there. And he was better than the other priest who used to wrestle altar boys to the floor, all for fun, and lay on top of us. Didn't he think we knew what was going on?

"And I was late going past the rectory because after school I helped Sister Mary Henry get the texts down from the top shelf of the closet." They'd buy that, how helpful I am. After all, around here I'm practically a servant. "It's these religious people, trying to get me to haul their crosses, that's what's keeping me after school. I should have called, I know, should have picked up the phone, but there's no phone in that classroom, the sister and I were working like devils, I didn't want to stop the progress, no telling how late she'd have had me working. Boy, am I beat! They don't let up, nuns and priests, they really crack the whip. I could have been there all night, hauling textbooks and then talking philosophy with Father Carey. Whew! Around this neighborhood they want your soul *and* your back."

They'd buy it.

Especially the old man who doesn't have great love of priests. He was dragged into the Catholic Church, since it's the only way the old lady would agree to marry him. He was raised Protestant, Lutheran, Episcopalian, Faithhealer, Psychic and a host of miracle cures for the soul that his mother bought and abandoned. A real mongrel. His impression is God has a thousand different masks, a regular Halloween party, you can get Him anywhere, as long as you have the cash. I'm not sure I agree with him. I'm not sure I don't.

Get him started on the Church and he's got a lot to say. And no telling what'll get him started. One day he was sitting in the front room chain-smoking his hatred of his job, his stomach sour, his breath putrid. The flowers wilted in our living room curtains. The walls yellowed. I couldn't tell what he looked like, through the haze, seated in a cloud of smoke, pouring his breath into the room. Smoke glued my eyelids when I blinked. He was trying to teach me to keep my eyes open, to endure. "All bosses are ass-suckers," he said, "They're fine people, family people to a man, but they get their jobs by stuffing their noses up the crack of the man who's sitting on them. And the man on them has his nose up the crack of the man above him, and so on. On the very top is the biggest hypocrite of all, the Pope, his nose is up God's ass. So there." He was my old man, I had to believe him. "Listen closely," he said, "I'm giving you the key to existence."

That's why I'm metaphysical minded and search for traces of God's tender bowels on the nose of every priest I see.

And keep my distance from the Church.

On days I don't work, I spend my time bouncing on the mildewed couch in the basement of my girlfriend's house, but I can't tell them that, the progress I'm making in the quest of love. "Well, I've got her bra unhitched now, one handed, I'm a smooth operator, a virtuoso, she lets me slide my finders along her belly, but still slams down the guillotine the instant I encounter a strand of hair." They wouldn't understand. I'm not sure I do.

But there's no need for excuses tonight. My sister is here with her arms out and the old lady is moving around us, where we hug, herding us away from lamps and ashtrays. No telling how passionate we'll get, brother and sister. She pushes a stack of newspapers under an end table. We could stumble, in our ecstatic dance to see one another, and crash against a painting, knock over a vase. Maybe it disappoints her we simply stand there with our arms around each other.

A flesh sister again. She isn't electricity, a static fouled voice in the telephone. She's home!

"Thank God!"

"It took me two days. I drove until I almost went off the road. In a ditch. At night. And it was raining."

"And a gorilla was beating on the side of the car."

"What?"

I laugh.

Her brown eyes are ringed with dark circles, her eyelids rimmed with blood. Her hair smells sweet, but her sweater is littered with crackers and ashes. She's here.

"Why didn't you call?"

"They wouldn't tell me when I was getting out. They made me wait. At the last minute I had to sign some papers and it was over."

She's beautiful. Slim. Her long brown hair, cropped short, but growing again, I can see it growing right before my eyes.

The old man sitting behind a newspaper kicks me in the knee when he uncrosses his leg, farts, grunts, "Merry Christmas."

Suddenly we're holding each other even tighter as the stench of growing up in that house overwhelms us . . . the overpowering brown odor of work mingled with the rot of things bought cheap and made to last that can't last . . . the sewage of long ago summer sticky on our skin as we shovel meat and potatoes in our mouths, in silence, sitting together, me in my half-price shirts, bargain basement pants, irregular socks, shoes chewed thin by the bite of old stained gravel, her flowered dress sewn and resewn and resewn and resewn . . . the old lady fluttering around the sink . . . the old man's flannel shirt rolled up, leaning on one elbow, looking down at his plate, forking it in, teaching us the horrible, unbearable, unavoidable rule of our life in one clear sentence, "Shut up and eat."

MOTHER:

Thing with having children is you have to encourage them all the time. You have to tell them what they need to do to get by in this life. How else are they going to know? When they need to do something, you have to encourage them to go out there and do it. In no uncertain terms. So they get it. Otherwise they'll think you're kidding and they'll sit around and not do anything. Or at least that's always been her problem. She's content to not do anything unless you encourage her. In no uncertain terms. So when she got back we started right away to encourage her to get a job. She was so tired from the drive from North Carolina. Her face was drawn and if it was up to me we would have sat around and talked about her Army experiences or this boy she was dating at the base, who sounded like a very nice boy, very good to her, or relatives, but Guy felt we should take first things first and encourage her right away to get a job. He was right, of course, that's the responsible thing to do. I don't know, though. She didn't react very well. She has all this resentment bottled up in her from the Army. She's like her father that way, and the two of them get an attitude and you can't talk. She acted mad that we were telling her what she could do next, but what are a mother and father supposed to do? We weren't telling her this for *our* good. It was for her. It's not easy being a mother.

"You're going to have to get a job."

"I know I have to get a job."

"Right away."

"Of course, right away."

"Do you know where?"

"I just got here. I don't know. I don't know what's out there yet."

"Well, where are you going to look?"

"I *don't know*."

"Start with the newspaper."

"Okay, of course."

"And then what?"

"I don't know."

"Start putting in applications."

"Well, what did you think I was going to do? Send them flowers?"

"Don't get smart with your mother."

"Honey, I want to make sure you know how to get started."

"All right."

"So where are you going to put in applications?"

"How should I know?"

"Well, start with the places you circle in the newspaper."

Yesss, Motherrrrr."

"Watch your mouth."

"Who's going to hire you with an attitude like that?"

She's a hardhead. Like her father. You can't get through to her no matter how patient you are. Nineteen years old you'd think she knows better what's expected of her. But she sits there with this look on her face that I'd like to wipe off with a slap. And she just got home.

I didn't have to be told when I was nineteen years old. I went out and got a job at the dimestore, because that was the smartest thing for me to do, have money of my own. I knew what had to be done and I went out and did it. I did pretty darn good for a high school dropout.

But she hasn't got any initiative and she's going to take some encouragement to get out there and work. She better get out there. I'll encourage her with a stick if I have to. Because I won't have her sitting around here, having boys over, stirring up dust, while we're at work. I had enough of that out of her when she was in high school, and it's about time she got up off her hiney and earned her keep.

You think I wanted to go back to work after I was married? After years of being sick in my female parts and with two kids to race after? But I couldn't stand watching him tie himself in knots over money, sit there gritting his teeth and glaring at us like we're robbing the blood out of his veins. I had enough to do wiping these kids' asses, but I saw what had to be done and I got up and did it. Guy didn't want his wife to work, no, he was going to put his foot down, but I made him drive me to beauty school every night after work, all the way to Royal Oak in the winter and I learned how to cut hair and give permanents and how to keep follicles from drying up and how to curl hair and wave it and color it. I learned everything there is to know about hair because I knew as a high school dropout I wasn't going to get a second chance. And then I went out and got a job.

I spent all day digging in dirty scalps. These women with their greasy, stringy hair, how I'd shampoo the filth out. You'd think they'd clean themselves before they let anyone else touch them, but they don't. God, the streaks on their necks. I'd find scabs that would come up under my fingernail, and bumps full of God knows what hidden here and there on their skulls. I'd find them while I was washing or combing, some of them so hard they didn't even move when I pushed on them. I was always afraid one of those bumps would pop open and get on me. It's very hard to do hair without touching a person. Some of these women I could feel my fingers curl when I looked into their puffy, fallen faces, but I had to do them. That's how you get money in the hair business, doing women you wouldn't touch with a broomstick. Besides, the tips piled up. I'd clink them into a metal baking soda can in the bottom of the dresser, and every Friday night I'd let the kids count it up. I'd take us all to dinner at the Rialto, fish dinner for a family of four, $5.79. I paid every penny. That was the first real luxury of my married life, the night once a week I didn't have to cook. It was almost worth a week of scrubbing scabby skulls.

When I went to work at Mr. Eddy's, they gave me the last chair by the bathroom and the radio. It always smelled when anyone went in there, and the radio was banging in my ear all day long. My nerves were shot, but I put up with it. Sometimes I'd come home from work at night and want to scream. I shut up and did my job. Mr. Eddy was pudgy and a little funny about women. Screechy about twice a day because someone didn't sweep up hair fast enough, or keep a comb clean, he'd throw his arms around and swear we were ruining him. He threw a hairbrush across the parlor once, hit a woman's purse as she was coming in, she turned around and walked right out again, and I don't blame her. Well, I had enough on my hands with Guy and his stomach and two screeching kids without putting up with that. When I was washing one of my regulars, Mr. Eddy came up and accused me of taking money out of the till, and the look on Elsa's face when she looked up at me with the suds around her face, like I was a filthy criminal, and I felt like I'd committed a mortal sin and I didn't do anything. Mr. Eddy apologized later, but what difference does that make? He'd made a mistake counting. So? So I still felt like I'd been caught stealing right out from under his nose. Every time one of the other girls looked at me, my hands would tingle. I wanted to cover my face. I kept my mouth shut, but I started looking for another job. I never let any grass grow on me. I got out of there and got busy in another place, which is what she's got to do.

And if she doesn't like one thing she's got to do another.

She doesn't want to be a steno. And she doesn't want to be a lab tech. Not that I blame her. I always thought it was awful to carry around jars of other people's urine and paper towels full of their feces for a living. Who would do that? She got a taste of it and wants to keep her hands clean. I had enough of doing hair, even after we spent all that money to send me to beauty school, three hundred dollars out the window. But I made it back. And Guy didn't look so tense for a little while. It wasn't all on his shoulders. While I was doing hair in the day, I went to business school at night and learned typing and shorthand and filing. I got my GED along the way. Once that door cracked open a bit, I didn't need much encouragement. I was on my way.

Office work is good. There's nothing I like better than cleaning up all the work on my desk. The only regret I have is that I couldn't be there for the kids when they came home from school.

BROTHER:

The day she went to work was the happiest day of my life, though I didn't realize it at the time. It got her out of here. It cleared the storm from the house, for a while. Then she'd come home shrieking. But that was all right. At least the job was sapping her vital energy, she didn't have as much left over to torment us. Though the little she had was more than enough. Kick off the shoes and start swinging. And make dinner at the same time.

"This house is a mess, a goddamn mess, don't you ever, ever leave your shoes in the middle of the floor like that again. What's this ashtray doing there? It goes here. Cut up some tomatoes, peel some potatoes!"

All hell broke loose. Dinner banged out. Boiled beef, boiled potatoes. Boiled carrots that made me shake my head with waves of nausea.

"Eat those carrots before I shove them down your throat!"

Beef so stringy I could have tied my shoes with it. Chewing it till it was a hard cud I had to wash down with milk. Action getting us to the table, silence fell when we sat. No talking during dinner; we still don't talk. We hunch over the table and scrape our plates clean.

"Shut up and eat."

Once when she was having trouble getting us settled down, we were goofing each other, crossing our eyes, giggling, she folded her hands on the table like she was going to say grace without us, but instead of "Bless us, oh Lord," she only said the first sound, trying to get us started, "Bllll . . ." and "Bllll . . . ," a motherly reminder. Hearing her made me laugh. It was ludicrous. I folded my hands in front of me and continued for her, "Blast us, oh Lord!" And he did. The old man knocked me right off my chair. I tumbled over backwards and lay on the floor listening to an angelic choir ring in my ears.

"Don't ever take the Lord's name in vain at this goddamn table. You understand?"

You'd think he believed in Jesus.

When she went to work, at least I could put my books down after school without getting clipped on the ear. She wasn't there to greet us at the door. What? No microscopic examination followed by a litany of wrongs? Sis and I actually started to get along for the first time. We relaxed, we watched TV, we ate crackers and called our friends on the telephone. We actually sat in the same room together. It was like the old days. Before we'd been separated, we used to take baths together, until I was four years old, slept in the same bedroom, played together. But the old lady figured my sister was getting too much of an education looking at me poked up out of the bath water (Slut!) and I'd begun to play with dolls (Queer!). Horror upon horror. Her children were disintegrating right before her eyes. They built a room on the back of the house and moved into it. I was put in a bedroom slightly smaller than a closet and my sister was shut into our former room, locked in, away from my prying five year old eyes. Kept covered. Kleenex stuffed in the keyhole. We weren't allowed to make tents together, because you-know-what happens when children are left unsupervised. I was sent outside to murder ants and tear up the flowers. She was sent to her room. I wasn't allowed to talk to her again until the old lady went to work.

She took to reading to us from the Bible every night. What a boon that was! What riches! She was going to get us on the right path, save us from the misfortune of childhood. Thank heavens she was there to guide us. And receive some guidance from the great Book for herself. Especially when she came across the part that said, "Spare not the rod." At last permission to save us! She knew how to do it. With me, at least. You don't touch a little girl in the same way. You have to be more subtle. But me? That was different.

I was beaten with a stick.

I was beaten with a belt.

I was beaten with a lint brush,
a broom handle,
an ice scraper
and a bamboo rake.

I was beaten with my father's hand,
my mother's hand,
my father's foot,
my mother's
and pounded on the head with knuckles by teachers who made me kneel down to take it.
They did it for my own good.

I was beaten with a shoe when I was late for dinner, but I hardly noticed what was happening.

I was beaten with fists
and kicked.
I lost a tooth.

I was beaten two swift hits and let go, and beaten until the old lady's arm was about to fall off.

I was beaten when she caught me and again after dinner when she told the old man.

I was hit on the back of the head, on the ass, on the ear, on the shoulder, on the chest, on the cheek, on the thigh, on the knee, on the foot.

There isn't too much of me that hasn't been beaten.

I've been slapped, swatted, punched, belted, booted (hilarious that one: the old man held my wrist, I ran in a circle while he booted me in the ass).

I was beaten lying down,
running past,
jumping up,
sitting still,
unexpectedly by the old lady, and deliberately by the old man who walked to my bedroom with heavy steps, told me exactly what I was going to get and then gave it to me.
He had a good reason.
So did everybody else.
I was silent,
though sometimes the cops came
because I screamed.

I was shaken so violently my head rolled on my shoulders, which was worse than the actual beating that followed.

I had to smell the belt.
I had to listen to it snap.

The old lady's spit flecked my face.

I was the third person, a ghost, "He thinks he can get away with that. Well, he's got another think coming."

I got beaten on the sidewalk and clipped on the lip,

cuffed,

cursed,

called, "Stupid,"

"Shithead,"

"Son of a bitch,"

and lots more that weren't my real name,

though I wasn't always sure.

But don't get me wrong.

I was lucky.

I never had to pray when they slapped me, like my sister did, to a statue of the Virgin.

That would have been intolerable.

Father:

I put a roof over their heads, food in their bellies, and covered their nakedness. They always had a pot to piss in. Even if half the time growing up my boy pissed everywhere but in it.

She cleaned it up.

"Get a nice even stream, boy, and aim right in the middle," I'd tell him.

The little son of a bitch couldn't hit the can. Too busy singing.

Fingersize pecker poked out of his britches, he'd sing to the birds out the window, piss running over the seat where he forgot to put it up. He didn't give a goddamn. Yodeled away with his dick flipping the best little piss-on-you attitude I ever saw.

MOTHER:

I looked at that door as long as I could. It just stayed there on its hinges and looked back at me. A big white door not moving every time I walked past it as I was getting ready for work. Like sticking its tongue out at me. What am I supposed to do, kneel down, worship at the altar of the Princess Fairy? That door getting under my skin as I'm running back and forth in front of it. Because I have to be at work. There's no easy path for me. I wish I had her life. I've got to be at my desk at 8:30 a.m. and ready to pick up that phone. That's why I get there at 7:45, so I make sure I have coffee made for the guys and a cup at my desk, and I have my day organized, my lunch put away, change my shoes into high heels that don't ruin on the cement outside, say hello to the guys as they come in. The other secretaries come in later, 8:30. No gumption. No get up and go. I'm always there ahead of them. If they followed my example and made a little effort, maybe they'd have my job, they could work for a big shot, and not these piddling so and so's they're stuck with. But they don't. They stroll in at 8:30, get their coffee, talk to each other, and they're not ready to work until almost 9. That's laziness. These executives need help right away. Sometimes the phone starts and doesn't stop all day, and I'm ready for it while they're still scrambling around like chickens trying to adjust their earrings and bras and everything. So I don't want hold ups in the morning. None. Everybody's got to get cracking. Period.

That's why that door really gets under my skin.

She's in there with her puffy face puffed up with sleep, that cave, in hibernation. Is she planning to sleep all summer? Time's a-wastin'. Under six covers in the middle of summer. Windows closed. I don't know how she can sleep in there in this heat with all those covers. Doesn't she have any blood circulation at all? Always been like that. Makes a cave for herself, a warthog cave she crawls into and you need a flashlight to see her under it. This is bad habits. The worst. I bet they didn't let her get away with that in the Service, and I'm not going to let her get away with it around here ever again. Fresh back, get things on the right track, that's the way I see it. She's not some kind of rodent that should stay in the dark away from everybody's eyes because it'll get stepped on if it comes out. She's a girl. A young woman. Who should be up and fresh-faced in the morning. That's how I was. I'd get up out of bed, when I was her age, with a song on my lips. I'd smile to everybody when I got up, because I was glad to be awake and see everybody first thing. Lucky us, we're all together. She takes after him. He's a grouch in the morning. First word out of his mouth is "Shit." From those cigarettes that have his lungs all clogged up with tar they're so sticky he can't get his breath out. And he smells his own breath. I'm sure that's why he's got that word in his mouth.

"Just once I'd like you to get up and say hello in a pleasant way, say what a nice day it is."

So he did. He got up one day and leaned over me in bed and said, "Great day in the morning. Wonderful to be alive, baby. Welcome to the bright, cheery wonder of a brand spanking new day, honey bunnykins." Sickening. I don't know what the answer is. He went into the bathroom and I heard him clear his throat and say that word. If he'd give up those cigarettes. You just have to look at the tar on the road to see that it's doing to his lungs, making them sticky so they pick up every fleck of filth in the air. No wonder he can't breathe. It leads to a bad attitude.

So I try first singing a little bit outside her door, something chirpy, "You gotta get up, you gotta get up, you gotta get up in the mooooorning," and tap lightly on the door. Makes me smile. There's a little stirring behind the door, a sound like crumpled paper being pulled out of a garbage can, maybe that's the covers moving. A grunt. I let it go. For a few minutes. I've got hair, make up, got to wash down the bathroom before I go to work.

But she's got to get up.

So the next time I walk by her door I make a little more effort to get her attention. I sing, louder this time, "Open up the gates leading to heaven!" and knock so I know she can't miss it even if she's in a deep sleep like the coma she's usually in.

Not even a grunt. She could have died in there. That paper

crumple sound, maybe that was suffocation, death rattle, so I open the door a little and her forehead is showing above the covers, her rat's nest spread all over the pillow. "Honey, honey, time to get up," and I flip the light to give her some encouragement and the covers come down a little and she looks up at me with one eye and moves her mouth open like she took a bite out of a dead squirrel, and rolls over with a long grunt that sounds to me like complaining.

I flip the light on and off and sing, "Time to get up" again.

"Mother."

"You've got to start looking for a job."

"The sun's not up."

"You don't want to be last in line."

"Jesus, Mother, this is only my third for Christ's sake day back."

"On the third day, she rose from the dead. I'll be back in five minutes. Be out of that bed."

I have to set a standard.

I bang on the door on the way out so she knows I've gone, but I rattle the doorknob when I walk past her door. To let her know I'm thinking about her. But I don't hear anything from in there. That big blank white door. Sitting there. So every once in a while I bang it with my fist, like a snooze alarm, every minute or so, to keep her awake. Because I don't know what she's thinking in there, what's keeping her so slow, is she asleep, awake, going for work, planning to sit around all day? What's going on behind her forehead? I bang again. And again. And again. And then I let a volley go that finally, *finally* gets a rise out of her.

"Yesssss, Mother."

She's sitting up on the edge of the bed curled over like all the bones in her back have given out, sucking, on a cigarette, looking at me with such a look.

Is this the little girl I raised?

FATHER:

Someone offers you a job you take the son of a bitch. Take anything. Get a job. You're gonna be under some man's thumb, so what? Get used to it. Think you can get married and not work for some man, think again. Married you're under his pecker, then you're working for him. Baking his bread, raising his brats. That's the way it is, honey. You'll work like the rest of us. Any job. Any fucking job that pays cash money is good enough. That got pounded in my head from the time I rolled out of my crib and I'm here to tell you it's the one sacred, honest to God truth I have found to be true in this life. You work. Someone offers you a job, you walk away from it, you're a peanut brain.

Doesn't matter you got to work for some son of a bitch stands over you on a ladder and pisses in your hair, you take the fucking job.

You want to talk to your grandfather. Some nights in the Depression all they had for supper was bread spread with lard. And he was a city cop. He had a job. Steady work. Have him tell you about the guys that had nothing. The only thing that separates you from dogs chasing up and down the alley knocking down garbage cans is you got a job. You lose it, start scavenging.

There's only one holy inviolate thing on this earth. One thing to make a religion out of if you know what's good for you. I'm talking about adoration, adulation and sending hallelujahs up past the power lines. The religion of *YOU GET A PAYCHECK EVERY TWO WEEKS*.

I have dropped on my knees and worn holes in my pants crawling under houses to install wires to keep this particular religion alive.

I have been baptized under God's almighty faucet in the sky when I was hanging by a belt from a pole, the electricity clicking under my fingers and lightening singeing the hair on my neck, in praise of this religious belief I have.

I have babbled litanies of "Yes, sirs," more abject than the lowliest plantation nigger because sometimes that's what it takes to keep the holy bread of life on the table.

I'm talking about PAYCHECKISM of which I'm the high priest of WORK TILL I GET IT.

So don't tell me you turned down what they offered. Ever. Not ever.

When the Lord said, "Abraham, you're gonna cut the heart out of your boy," what He meant was Abraham's going to offer up his son to some boss somewhere, because that's what he's got to do, and will always have to do, and that is the way of the Lord, that some son of a bitch boss is gonna cut the heart out of his boy and there ain't no angel to hold back the knife. That boy'll grow old before his time and when his hour is upon him, he'll have a weary, but happy smile on his kisser as he jumps feet first into an early grave to get some goddamn rest.

But at least he'll eat along the way if he sticks to the religion of YOU GET A PAYCHECK EVERY TWO WEEKS.

Now, honey, it's no different for you, me, your mother or your brother. So you get out there and start putting in applications. And be happy to get something because there's nothing out there. No job is too mean. None of us are too good to do what we have to do. Because we're working stiffs.

Some people are born with a silver spoon in their mouth and they got someone there to wipe their ass every time it unpuckers. Well, we're not that lucky.

We were born to do the wiping.

SISTER:

"Christ, of all the rotten luck, shit, I can't believe this no good motherfuckergoddamnittohellpiss job I got. Why's this happen to me? I put in one application. One! This sleaze bag company on Mt Elliot looks like they're going to close down on Tuesday and this fat wheezing sleaze bag in white shoes blows smoke in my face and says I start next week. This city is supposed to be going down the tubes. What's going on? You can't count on anything.

"It's first that they don't let up at home. They have a cattle prod in my back. And the lectures. You should hear my father go. I want to say, 'All right. All right. I got the idea. You want me to squat on the throw rug in my bedroom and play dolls, right? No? Gee, I'm confused. I get the impression you'd like me to go through the refrigerator and eat till I'm three hundred pounds and then you'll be glad to go get me some Fritos and ice cream. No? Well, what exactly is it you expect from me? It's a little vague. Something about a job. That is, you don't ever want to see your little girl sully her well tended nails with the vulgar buffoonery of labor.' (That's what this guy I used to date in the Service called it.) 'Oh,' I want to say, 'Oh, I think I got it. You *do* want me to adopt this particular buffoonery. *You* want *me* to get a *job*. Me. You're not talking to someone behind me, are you? You mean *me*. Yes, you're right. Your fingers pointing at me two inches from my nose is a tip off. I am the only one sitting on the couch, yes, I got it. You do mean me. This is shocking. A revelation. I mean I never expected this from you two.'

"I'm telling you, Janet, you wouldn't believe the way they go about telling me how to get it. I want to pull out my second grade graduation certificate and say, 'Look, folks, I'm over qualified for these instructions you're giving me.' The only way they could be any more specific is if they drill a little hole, no, it'd have to be a big hole to be clearer, a big hole in the top of my head and pour in their vast worldly knowledge.

"So here's to my first week at work. Drink up. It's stupid. A bunch of women in a typing pool. A desk every six feet and heaps of paper on the left the salesmen put down—wait'll I tell you about Tom, he's one of my salesmen—and then we type them up, no mistakes, and this other girl makes sure they get back to the salesmen and a copy to Mr. Edwards, who checks them. When I roll back my chair I hit right into the chair of the girl behind me. And we're not supposed to talk, just sit there all day, staring at our stupid typewriters. But everybody talks when Mr. Edwards goes into his office. He'll come out into the doorway and look at us if we get too loud, but so what? He looks like he has paper clips under his eyelids. I figured his wife must look like a bag of leaves, a big bumpy brown bag full of wet leaves, and smell like it, too. He has a paunch that would pitch an ordinary man on his face, but fortunately he's got a butt to balance it. A butterball man like him needs a big bag full of leaves to get on top of. But in his office is a picture of his wife, who's small and pretty, almost pretty, with their son, which proves someone climbed someone in bed, at least once. I'd put my money on her. Climbing Mount Edward. Have to. He'd crush her.

"On my second day he threw a bunch of papers that would have hit me if I didn't have my purse in front of me on the desk. Then he turned around on his heel, stiff, like he had a pencil up his what-sis. And not the eraser end. The papers were scribbled all over in red like I was in school all over again, and smeared so much with circles and helpful comments like, 'This will not do,' I couldn't even correct on them, but had to start over.

"I could have walked right then. But I didn't know what's worse, him, or going home and telling them I quit my job.

"Which is when Tom comes walking over, picks up the papers, which happened to be his, and lifts his eyebrow. We'd had a couple of looks back and forth that day already. And I'm here to tell you, Janet, if I had to rate this guy's buns on a scale one to ten, I'd give him a little pinch, right underneath the tuck part of his buns. Mmmm.

"He picks up the papers and says, 'That's it. That's it. I can't work under these conditions,' loud so the whole office is stopped dead. Then he looks at me, and leaning over my desk says, 'Look at this. Look. How am I supposed to use these.'

"Mr. Edwards comes barrelling out of his office set to suck blood out of someone's heart. 'Wha . . . Wha . . .'. He's too excited to even get a whole word past his flaps, and his gut is jiggling, and I believe he had so much blood moving in his body, his pants were visibly throbbing.

"'Mr. Edwards, I cannot, will not, refuse and simply won't work like this. Sir, I tender my resignation. I quit and I'm going over to Banyon's.' That's the other place down the street.

"Edwards is running out, 'Wha . . . Wha . . .,' right at my desk I thought he wouldn't be able to stop. A locomotive. It was threatening. A lawsuit in the making.

"Tom says, 'Mr. Edwards, I don't care this new girl makes a typo or two or three. What's it matter? I don't want to frame these, just need to read them.'

"My jaw's dropping, I'm thinking, 'Oh, boy, here's another asshole going to sink me in shit.'

"'But look what this new girl has done. Loops of red ink so I can't possibly read them. Writing her personal notes up and down the page. It's revolting. It's stupid. It's inefficient. You'd need an IQ of three to do something like this. Mr. Edwards, why in heaven's name do you let her get away with it? I've got too much to do. I can't be playing games with deciphering through her red ink. I insist you either take away her red pens or I walk right now. This minute. Going, going . . . I'm gone, sir, I'm gone!'

"By now everybody is catching on because Mr. Ed, fat old horseface, red ink is his trademark. He gapes, can't believe he's hearing this. Then he says, 'Get back to work, Petrocelli,' and walks back to his office with that stuck up roll to his butt.

"Come to find out Tom's the number one salesman, twenty-five years old, and he laughs and says, 'I got the old man's testicles in a test tube and every so often I like to put them on the Bunsen burner to keep him alert.' He's a funny guy and he took me out for a drink after work."

"Anything happen?"

"Nothing much."

"Nothing much what?"

"We went to a bar on Jefferson. He knew everybody and introduced me around."

"Then what?"

"Nothing. Really, not that much happened."

"Kiss him?"

"Janet."

"Kissed him and . . . and . . ."

"Well . . . not that much."

"C'mon. Handjob?"

"All right. Handjob."

"Oh, you disgusting pig. How could you? Hung?"

"The whole salami."

"First date you're grabbing him."

"He's grabbing me. He wouldn't drive me back. He said we'd sit in the parking lot all night if we had to."

"Really."

"Yeah. It took the edge off for me. For me it was like a handshake."

"A handshake, for Christ's sake."

"Yeah, but the hand only had one finger. One very long, fat finger. Salami ala King."

"Second day you're screwing the office."

"I didn't screw him. He's nice. Tomorrow he'll be there. And I got to go back to the grind. Shit, Janet, I didn't collect one goddamn unemployment check. Not one. Do you believe that?"

BROTHER:

The executioner, the Gestapo, the way the old lady is beating on that door again, an early morning raid, going to drag her into the street by the hair and shoot her in the face, in front of the neighbors, no, not in the front of the neighbors, in the garage, so the neighbors can guess when they hear the shots being fired what's going on in that house, what the hell are they doing over there, what mysteries are hidden behind the calm front of that house? You'd think she'd worry about waking the neighbors, beating that way on her door, but there's nothing self-conscious about it, a couple of taps, then heavy banging, doorknob rattled, the light switch clicked on and off, yelling, singing. I don't even have to guess, the sound is so clear. I can lay up here and watch it unfold.

It's her skin, my sister's door, the skin she could never protect from them. She was getting grabbed and jerked around, "Look at me when I'm talking to you," or her jaw pinched in the old lady's hand, "Wipe that look off your face when I'm talking to you," or her hair pulled back and her head in place while the old lady combed it, harsh pulling strokes that had tears welling in her eyes, "Look at this mess, don't you ever comb it, don't you have any pride?" The door is her skin. She stays behind it for as long as she can. Like a burn victim, no skin left of her own, so she has an artificial barrier between her and the rest of the family, the rest of the world. The door is hard and reverberates with pounding, but if she covers her ears and scrunches down under the covers, far under the covers, then she doesn't have to listen to it. If she sinks into sleep deep as death, then she doesn't even have to hear the knocking, that persistent awful pounding that goes on for an hour in the morning, because the old lady isn't about to let her sleep in, past starting time, for her job, or anybody else's job.

My sister would like to carry that door around with her, on her shoulders, and talk to everyone through it, the better to protect herself, peek around it like a crazy person on the street. She would put doors around her desk at work if she had a choice, and wear doors like sandwich boards on the street, and have a door with a little window on it to put between herself and her dates when she's out driving to the restaurant with them, so she can open the little window and talk, maybe kiss, but the door is too small for them to fit a whole hand through, and too small to see her completely, so she can hide behind it, and not be known, be safe. Be safe.

"Come out, come out wherever you are," the old lady sings outside the door, like a cheerful cat trying to lure out the mouse. But there are teeth in that mouth really saying, "Come out, come out and be eaten." She knows that. She knows there's saliva dripping from incisors and if she walks out her bedroom door she'll be scrambling between two gigantic paws that will play with her a bitter game of Chew On You. So she hides behind the door and sinks into a sleep just this side of never to awaken.

She has three alarm clocks to call her when she absolutely has to get out of bed, the last possible minute: One on her nighttable, which she flips down on the floor, fumbling for the off button, another across the room on a shelf by the window that she's got to get out of bed to turn off, and another windup clock inside her closet she has to get out of bed and find before she can turn off. She sleeps so deeply she can silence all three, crawl under her covers and never have stepped out of her dream.

The old lady won't be dismissed so easily. Furious at the white skin of that door, she beats her knuckles raw. Then her heavy heels hammer the floor into the kitchen. Pans and pot rattle, clanging on the counters, in the sink. Thumps her way down the hall, again to beat on that door. She gets her up, she raises the dead woman from her bed and sends her out into the world with her hands still numb, her soul still burrowing in the mattress.

MOTHER:

I don't know why he would say those things. I don't know what he's getting at, saying those things, that don't have to be said. Not ever. Encourage. Encourage. Encourage. That's the best way. That's what I always do. But he's got to make a point out of everything. Sticks his fork in the kids' faces makes a point out of everything, thinks he's the only one in the whole world that can figure out what to do on this earth. We all been making our way. I wanted to throw the whole plate of city chicken in his face and hope those little wooden sticks stuck in his cheek. That's how mad I got. Forgive me, awful way to think. But he gets me so mad I could spit. She got a job, okay? She got a job so lay off, okay? Let her go off to work every day and get some money behind her. But that's not good enough for him. He's got to make a point out of it. A priest is what he should have been, if he believed in God more, so he could stand on a pulpit and raise hell telling everyone what to do. Father Guy. Saint Guy. Sticking his finger in everybody's face and making a point.

He says, "You got a job, okay? So what? So what?"

"So nothing," she says, "It's what you wanted. So I got one. What do you mean?"

"You only got one because I told you to."

He was setting a trap I knew it. She knew it. She looked at him. He had a mouthful of city chicken pushing out the side of his face, and a forkful of mashed potatoes he was aiming at her.

"So you got a job. What's that make you?"

"Nothing. I don't know. Working. Employed."

"First word. First word was it. Nothing. It makes you nothing. Until you make something of it."

I got up and went to the sink because I couldn't sit there and watch him do this to the kids. Why's he do it?

"How much did you make today, boy?"

Looking at Mark who was daydreaming again. Get the meal over with, I think, and spoon another can of applesauce in the bowl.

"Not much."

"How much?"

The boy's job at a motel on Jefferson, yardboy. A few after school dollars.

"Five bucks, maybe."

"Five! Five! You go all the way downtown for five bucks. You work hard?" The boy nods. "You worked hard for that five bucks, tell me you did, right?"

"Yeah, I worked hard, sort of hard."

He turns to her, drops the fork on his plate, folds his arms on the table like he's just got to know something from her, and asks, "What'd you make today?"

"I don't know."

"You don't know, you don't know what you made. Did you make anything at all? You getting paid for this labor you're providing, or is this public service, something for the good of the community, this so-called job you got."

"I got paid."

"What?"

"Three eighty-five an hour."

"Four bucks, say, four bucks an hour. You made thirty-two dollars today, less, all day working, and you think that makes you something. Thirty-two bucks."

"I didn't say it made me anything. I didn't say anything."

"That's something. Only thirty-two dollars and the boy here made five bucks. And your mother, I'll tell you, I'll tell you what your mother made, about fifty bucks. Now there's a lesson for you here and I want you to pay attention to it. Don't get that look on your face. Listen and learn something. You got to stay steady on a job to get anywhere, stay at it and then you get somewhere. Because until you're there you're nothing. You got that? I been twenty years working for these sons of bitches at Edison. I'm not saying I'm something, but I'm more than you are. So you can judge what I'm saying. Five bucks, thirty-two bucks, fifty bucks, comes to eighty-seven bucks. Now that's a belly laugh if I ever heard one."

He's getting me mad. He's telling them what I make and he's

making it small and I worked to get where I am today. The boy's eating faster, trying to get out before it leads anywhere he doesn't want it to go.

"Eighty-seven dollars is chicken shit. Nothing. I'll tell you I went to my job today and I got home ahead of all of you, and what'd I get for it? For eight hours. Same hours as you. Same as your mother. That's for working, yeah, I worked, I didn't sit on my duff, but what'd I get? I made over a hundred dollars today. That's just today. That's some money. Nobody at this table is getting rich on it, but that's some money for a working stiff to count on every day of the week. In other words, I made more than all three of you combined. By myself. That should tell you something."

I didn't know what it was supposed to tell her, what it told any of us. I put the cookie jar on the table. Get the meal over with.

"I got a crummy job, okay?"

"It's not a crummy job. You just got to make it into something."

"I don't want to stay there the rest of my life."

"Then you're going to start at the bottom all over again. If you haven't got any steadiness. You're gonna be making thirty-two dollars the rest of your life. You want that? Is that what you want to be making the rest of your life? Thirty-two dollars that I gotta say makes you about as important in the world as a pimple on a flea's pecker."

"I only been there six weeks, what am I supposed to get in six weeks?"

"You'll get a raise in six months like they said, if you last six months, if you're not starting over as a thirty-two dollar pimple before six months is over. And I'm going to tell you how you can do that."

"Oh, brother."

"You get your ass in bed on work nights so you can get up in the morning. By yourself. I'm sick of your mother having to come in there with a chair and whip to chase you out of your den. What are you doing out there that keeps you out half the goddamn night? That's some overtime. That *was* overtime, wasn't it? You're not out there doing anything you'd be ashamed of in the confessional, are you? You got a bed to be in and you'll find it in the back of this house. You got that? You got that? Or you're going to stay a thirty-two dollar pimple."

It gets mixed up. I thought I knew what he wanted to say, about keeping the job, then he tells her she's staying out late. Her face is curdling, bunching around her mouth, means they're going to start again, start back where they were before the Service. Then Mark sneezes and sprays germs all over the table. Well, I tell him how I feel about that, do it loud, bat him on the shoulder to cover his mouth, thinking this will get everybody's mind off her nights out.

Him and her are still glaring at each other. Her face between spit in his eye and tears running down, tears like when she was twelve years old and I'd hold her and she'd say, "He hates me. He hates me," and I'd say, "No, honey, he doesn't," and I don't think he did then, but sometimes I'm not so sure. He goes about making her feel like this, tells her she's nothing, and I think sometimes she gets so mad because she doesn't want to be nothing any more, even though she's young and can't really be anything else yet.

And then he scrapes his chair back on the linoleum and it doesn't matter I told him to be careful of the floor, or maybe that's why he isn't careful of it, to make a point to me, same point as the plate we have hanging on the kitchen wall that says, THIS HOUSE IS MY HOUSE AND I'LL DO AS I DAMN WELL PLEASE, and he crumbles his napkin and rolls it in the gravy on his plate. Or maybe he scrapes his to make a different point, says, "This isn't your house, this is my house and you're all in the way, and you're all nothing. Nothing," and leaves the table blowing air out between his lips just this side of blowing up, so we're left looking at each other. Mark's in the cookies, but with a look on his face he's stealing them. I'm pulling plates off the table now fast as I can because the sooner we get out of the kitchen the better.

He's in his chair reading a filthy magazine and that's saying the same thing as that plate on the wall, "This is my house and if I want to invite these naked women in, I'll do it," not thinking what it's like to have them in our house.

"I feel like looking at naked broads in a magazine, I'll look. It's what I want to do and that's the end of it."

"How do you think that makes me feel, you looking at that right here in our living room, in front of me. How am I supposed to feel?"

"You want me to hide? Go out in the alley and pretend I'm

ashamed of them? I'm looking at them, not you. What's it got to do with you? I'm not touching. You got the only ass these hands touch, baby. I start to wander, I start sniffing the neighborhood, you got a problem. Meanwhile, I look at what I want to look at."

"What's it make our daughter feel like, growing up with you reading these magazines?"

"Makes her feel like her old man's normal. I live in a great big world. A sexual world, baby. I got eyes in my head. Some broad wants to show me her bare ass in a magazine least I can do her is the courtesy of looking. Half the world, one out of every two people in the world, one of them's got a furry little moneymaker. If you're a man, you've got to look unless you're a queer in a pink tutu. You fill the front of your Jockey shorts, then you look. She's gonna know her old man is a man. I'm not going to hide it or pretend I'm anything different. You got a problem with me being a man, you don't like me being a man?"

"I didn't say that. That's not it."

"You think I'm running around?"

"No, of course not."

"You think I'm *thinking* of running around? Wrong. You keep me satisfied, honey, you got nothing to worry about. No broad in a magazine is going to turn my head."

"Why do you do it then?"

"I do what I want to do."

He says he's got enough with me, and if he's got enough with me, what's he find there? Does it wake him up? Can he talk to them? He can't talk to a magazine, and it's paper with none of the warmth a husband and wife have. Maybe it's nothing, like he says, and it doesn't mean anything and he only does it because he does it. But then why doesn't he do something that means something to him. Read about the Civil War or sports, something he gets something out of, instead of something he says he gets nothing out of, unless maybe he does get something out of looking at naked women. But what?

The telephone makes the whole room jump, like someone standing on the sidedrive lifted the curtain and looked in on us and heard everything we were saying, everything we were thinking, frowned and clapped his hands hard.

"I got it," Mark snatches the phone before she can get it, and says, “It’s for you. It’s a boy,” and she tears it away from him because the boy on the line can hear everything. She pulls the cord across the kitchen and sits on the basement stairs, one step from the back door. And I know out that back door is where she’s going. I can hear it in her sweet voice, but I don’t know where she’s going after she goes through it.

I don’t know.

But I know I taught her to keep her clothes on. And that’s something.

SISTER:

The thing I like best, that makes me feel best, that keeps making me do it, is they stop being mean to me when I take my clothes off. I think sometimes it's because I have something to drink all the time when I'm sitting there talking to them that makes it feel good. But it's not. Not that. Not the drink. It's when I take my clothes off they talk to me and you can see that what they have to say they say right to me at that moment and no one else. Low and dirty talk sometimes, but nice, too, that comes welling from deep inside them, some of them so sincere it's like tears welling up out of their stomach, these low voices. They lean against me so hard they glue against me, and whisper in my hair, how my hair catches their words and hangs on to them.

There's Tom that wouldn't even look at me after a couple of days in the office, think I never existed after that first. I'd position myself around at my desk so I could face him, but try not to make it too obvious when he came in, that I wouldn't mind another night, but he was so busy he'd hustle through, talk to the other girls, or drop paper on my desk so fast and be gone that I didn't have time to blink before I was looking at his back, and that was the meanness of silence. Him freezing me out and I couldn't tell at first that's what it was, as if he was embarrassed by what took place between us, or if I wasn't any good and so he like blew his nose on me and now was going to throw me away, or at least that's how it felt. And being thrown away like dirty Kleenex isn't any bath can wash that off, and so I'd get this catch in my throat every time he walked out without stopping to kid with me. Did he have someone else all the sudden, or didn't he like me, or did I do something wrong? I must have done something really wrong to get frozen like that from him, like dirty Kleenex, but then Janet and me went to the bar and I started talking to another guy that he'd introduced me to before, and Tom came in, walked up to this guy to talk to him before he noticed me, and we ended up talking most of the night, and at first he was slow to come toward me, but when I didn't appear mad and was still offering, the silence stuttered away, we had a few drinks, and by the time he was pulling my blouse out of my skirt, the meanness was gone replaced by something direct at me that it couldn't be anything *but* for me.

Why is it they don't notice me? I don't even exist. I think they're blind or have their minds so confused with baseball or cars that they don't see what's in front of their eyes, but when I take off my clothes and lie down where they can see me, they see. Their eyes get full of me and I know if there's taste in their eyes, they're tasting, and pretty soon they're tasting all over me.

Jack was the meanest of them, but I fell in love with him the most. Everything was mean about him in the way he talked about me, and treated me, and I was supposed to clean up after him and cook for him and take his mean jokes in front of people like I was his wife and should sit there and be showered with abuse. He's the one that got deepest to me and I couldn't let him go, had to have him, until finally I left because the Service was over and he didn't want me there without paying some of the apartment. He'd grab me and push me around but when I took my clothes off, then it was another matter. He'd look at me, and when I said something to him, he heard exactly what I said, and would talk directly at me, didn't, couldn't ignore me when he was there naked and I was naked. Even then he'd say things wrong, but through it, the meanness melted away, mostly.

And I think sometimes wouldn't it be better instead of nodding and being polite when men and women met, wouldn't it be better if we took our clothes off right there, I'd say, "Tom, this is Janet. Janet, this is Tom," and they both would drop their clothes to the floor and start running their hands over each other like blind men over the elephant, trying to figure out what they got here, what is this, my oh my, and this, and then they wouldn't have to start with the meanness, but get right away to the good part. That would be better. A little rough in winter. But the payoff in the long run would be worth a few sniffles. A case of pneumonia.

Because there's so much meanness.

And I think sometimes my father is the meanest of all of them. Glad I'm not my mother. It doesn't even help him to look at those magazines of his. The meanness is still settled over his face like a spill. You'd think he was looking at pictures of disease and bloated children and somebody's puke the way he scowls, but maybe it's because I don't know him, maybe he's no meaner than Jack, but I don't see him the way my mother does. And I don't think that I want to, even though that might clear up the mystery.

And if the way to get past the meanness is the way I said, maybe that's why it seems like lately I've been trying to get past the meanness as fast as I can.

There was a guy at the restaurant where my cousin waits tables the other day said hello, and I'd been there for a couple of hours already talking to Susie when she got little breaks, sitting at the bar, but in a couple of minutes it seems like this guy and me were holding each other, he was rubbing my neck and we were perched on stools with our arms around each other kissing in front of everybody and what's more, what amazes me, is that I'm the one that touched him first, and I didn't realize that until this morning, but I'm the one that put my hand on his shirt and gave him the courage. Because I don't think he had the courage. I didn't want to sit there and have to go through all the remarks, didn't want to have to go through getting to know him, having him turn from nice to mean, uncover him, find out the meanness. I wanted to jump right to the good stuff, was that so bad?

There was a teacher I had who read a poem to us, from a skinny book that a woman wrote, and it had a line in it, went, "She runs naked through the trees, yelling: touch me. Touch me." A couple of people giggled when she read that. Most everybody passed over it. But I scribbled it down and thought, 'That's me, that's me she wrote about,' because of how much better it gets when that happens, you get touched.

But it makes it hard to go home sometimes.

I can't go home until the eleven o'clock news is over and the lightbulbs are cold. I can't walk through that living room with them in it. I let myself in long after they've gone to bed and step softly, trying to miss the sounds in the floor. The streetlight throws enough light to see spooks in their chairs, his large, made of smoke, even bigger than he is, glaring at me as I walk past the chair, and her's, fainter, turned toward his, sitting there talking to him.

Their bedroom door is closed and I hear him snoring, but their ghosts here in the living room judge how well I combed my hair after I left some guy, how primly I tucked in my blouse. Walking through the living room makes me sweat and sick to my stomach worse than if they were here in person. I can't fight the ghosts, whose eyes follow me from the instant I push back the front door. The pictures on the wall, the furniture, the lamps found places years ago, and they never move. A comfortable tomb, a shadow world for these ghosts stiff with anger, waiting.

No pleading with them. I didn't mean to, I didn't want to go back to the guy's place, it was the only place to go, when I couldn't sit in the bar any longer and I couldn't sit in his car, and I couldn't come back here until the lightbulbs were cold.

The steel screens don't come out easily and the windows are narrow, only a burglar the size of a jockey could squeeze through, not these hips, otherwise I'd climb in the back, not so they don't know what time I got home, but so I can get to my room, the quiet of it, without going past the ghosts.

BROTHER:

He never should have said something like that out loud. Never. If he thought it, okay, he thought it, but he should keep it to himself because when he said it, it infected me in the ear. And no matter how hard I try to get rid of it, I can't. That's why I wish he'd just shut up. Please, God forgive me, I want to stuff his mouth with a gasoline rag and burn those words out. I can't loosen them from my ears.

It makes me hate him.

The old man ranting, "There's only one reason a girl comes crawling back to the barn at four in the morning. She's got round heels."

"Guy, for Christ's sake, that's no way to talk about your daughter."

"If you're gonna talk, you tell the truth, don't you? She's flat-backing. Find some other excuse for her coming in at that hour."

"I don't want to hear that."

"You gonna shut your eyes and plug your ears and stick your head in the sand, maybe you can come up with a different conclusion. I can't. That's how I see it. I don't know where she learned to behave that way, but it's nothing we done around here. We tried to teach her, but I guess it don't do no good when the merchandise is haywire to begin with."

"We did try to teach her."

"She's a goddamn hardhead like her old man."

"But for Christ's sake, we don't have to talk about it."

"It don't matter if I say it because if I don't you're gonna say it. And if you don't say it, he's gonna say it. And if he says it, it won't come as a surprise to you because you thought it already and I thought it already."

I never thought it, he's wrong. I never thought it. She's not like that and won't be like that. I want to light that rag and watch his whole head go up in flames.

"I never thought it."

"You thought it, boy, because you're part of this family. You thought it because you don't have a thought that's your own. It all belongs to the family. You think you got your own thoughts, but what *I* think comes out *your* mouth. What I say, you thought first. We're a family, we're one way of thinking, one way of talking. That's it. We're like green shit you see in a swamp. They tell you it's a billion little crawly things living together. But you look at it, take the evidence of your eyes. It's all one green shit. Whether you like it or not, we're like that. We speak with one voice. There's a lot less difference between you and me than you want to believe."

"Your father's trying to say we all have the same family heritage."

"I'm trying to say we're all the same fucking bacteria."

I never thought it. Now he's said it, I can't stop thinking it. Damn him. Filth is what his words are. They spray in the air and infect it, long after he forgot what he said, because it didn't matter that much to him, it can't matter or how could he go on living with her under the roof. The words stay there, living things, floating in the sea of air, and get inside you. They crawl up and down your skin and sift through your pores. I'm not like them, not either one of them. I don't look like them. I don't think like them. I have a different nose and my eyes are not like anything ever seen in the family before. Brown eyes, but a different shade of brown than anything that's ever been, a little darker, I think a little darker. I'm not them. But he sprays words in the air like a filthy sneeze, it hangs there, washes over me. When I walk through the room, it clings to me.

Her voice telling me she doesn't do things like that with men and I believe her. And I believe her because if I have to believe someone it's going to be her. And I must believe either the old man or her. Because the way he says it, either she does do things with men, or she doesn't. There's no middle ground. It's either yes or no. Up or down. This way or that. Make a choice. The old man always says, if you don't think this, then you think that. No prisoners are taken in this house. Say the right thing or you are the enemy. You will be shot. We demand an opinion. A or B. The old lady, either you're clean or you're dirty. You're either polite or a pig. There is no indifference. Choose! You're either overcoming sickness or falling into it. You're either on time or you're late. And every choice has consequences, dire consequences. If I'm on time, I love my mother. If I'm late, I've obviously gone out of my way to hurt her. If I say, Yes, my sister does things with men, then I choose the old man, and I must sneer at her and abandon her.

He shouldn't say things like that. It poisons the air. It's hard to breathe.

Her voice. Not lying.

"I don't do those things, it's disgusting."

Of course, I believe her. Because I can hear in her voice she's telling the truth.

Now to the old man I'm worse than a traitor. I'm a fool.

CHAPTER THREE

THE PERFECT SATURDAY

FATHER:

I don't know what it is with women. It's like they got a hinge so all a man's got to do is tweak their knee and they squeak open. The squeak is a little cry of protest, but it doesn't mean much. I only met one any different, so I married her. And that was exactly the right oil to get her hinge working. But not before. Sweating and straining, showered and shaved, sober and perfumed, I couldn't move her knees. Traveled the whole world and never met a pair of knees with such iron clad lock up and it drove me insane. I'd go to sleep at night toting an iron rod I could have used as a crowbar, and in the morning I had to leave my pants unbuttoned for half an hour until it decided to give me some peace.

And I don't know where it came from with her. Every other woman I ever met had an easy way about her, a sign like a billboard around her neck that flashed on and off neon whenever I came over to visit, said, "I'm yours for the asking," but I wanted one I could be sure of when I went to work. I made the right choice. I got the only woman cleaner than the Virgin Mary. Except maybe my own mother, the original Puritan Enforcer. The only way she agreed to have children was if my old man left a thimble of sperm outside the bedroom door. She'd put it where it had to go. Sex was a necessary evil to have children, so I know she was never catting around. Hell, she never even left her bedroom door unhitched. She'd have posted a guard if we could afford it. The old man had to knock like a house guest. And that's how she treated him, a long term visitor that had started to smell after three days like a bucket of smelt. It says a lot about his tenacity that he got six children, five live ones, out of her, unless he forced her down with a revolver, but I wouldn't know anything about that.

None of my sisters inherited my mother's purity. As soon as a rug grew on their split, they put it to use. There was enough mewing under our windows to give a dead man the jitters. Every neighborhood boy that could find his zipper strayed to our house. My mother was out there with a broomstick half the nights of the week to shag them out. The other nights of the week, of course, she rode it.

I got two lazy sisters and two crazy ones. But it's hard to tell who's who because they're all more or less lazy and crazy. Hung with jewelry, they got dispositions that'd melt granite, hot and nasty. The boys heard the clatter of their beads, they'd start to salivate, but by the time they got done with them, the boys would whimper back to their mommas, skinned to the bone. They got fat early and liked to roll around the couch when no one was home, with a preference for skinny boys like me, slight of stature, that they could toss around like pizza. Any boy unlucky enough to get tagged with the fatness that turned into one of my nieces or nephews now enjoys the proud privilege of being my brother-in-law. What a sorry crowd of faces that is.

So I don't have to wonder where the girl got it from. Straight down my side. We did everything to teach her different, telling her how to keep herself clean for a husband, how to land one in the first place, but she has blood that traces straight back. And you can't fight blood with words. Conniving female blood that misses a female every once in a great while like my wife, but gets every other one. I had hopes that my daughter could have that same pure streak in her, but it turns out she's like all my sisters and there's no stopping it, no denying it, and the sooner I admit it, take her for what she is, the better off I'll be.

Maybe that's why it pisses me off so much when I blow my cork. Night after night hearing the floor bend as she creeps home. And that goddamn pig sty she leaves when we haul her ass out for work in the morning. I looked in there and there's a vase on her vanity with a limp flower draped over the side of it, the water couldn't be water, no goddamn way, it's got to be piss in there, it's so yellow, and brushes piled up with rats she pulled out of her head and combs on the floor. The ashtray is the only clean thing on the counter because the ashes are spilled on the rug. There's Kleenex everywhere smudged with lipstick, make-up, probably a few pimples squeezed in there, maybe she's wiping her ass and throwing that on the floor, too, or wiping something worse. But the thing that gets me as I'm standing there is the screwdriver on the dresser top I been looking for for two weeks. Once something goes in that room it's good as flushed down the toilet. You're lucky to see it again. My fucking screwdriver. She knows to put back what doesn't belong to her. And she used it to dip into one of her ointments or lotions because the end of it is covered with shellack and stuck to the dresser top. The varnish pulls away when I pick it up and I'm so goddamn mad at that moment I kick the covers hanging off the side of the bed, and goddamn if I don't clip a kitchen plate she hid on the floor under the bed with my toe. It skids across the room and cracks on the closet door.

And she's out on a so-called date.

By now my mouth is out of control the whole house is alert.

She's up from the basement with a basket of laundry in her arms, standing in the door of the bedroom, and the boy flicks his head past, not about to stop. Red is what I'm seeing. I run my arm across the top of the counter and send bottles and jars, magazines, flower petals, letters, stuffed animals in a shit pile on the floor. A crash of shit and cloud of dust. Hi-Yo, Silver! My flannel shirt has a line of filth along it gets me madder. The vanity, same thing. Right in the middle of the room.

She's saying something, but why stop? The fun's just beginning.

The drawers half pulled out I yank the rest of the way, rumble them on top of the heap. The broken dish. Toss it in. There's a curtain hanging half off its rod, comes down easy enough and then I flip her bed, nest of stray hair and sweat stain, dirty sweat shirt, a wet washcloth—why the fuck's a washcloth in the bedroom?—and two nighties, flip it on the whole mess. Take the wastebasket piled to overflowing and empty it on top of the mattress.

The screwdriver I keep.

Put it in my back pocket and sit in the front room with the paper. She doesn't say anything. I can hear the boy's record player upstairs. I know I was damn mad because I sat there reading not a word I held in front of my face, and it's an hour before I realize that screwdriver poked through my pants, is sticking up my ass, going to give me a sore cheek for a month.

She brings up the towels from the dryer, folds them on the couch. The snap of the towels brings me around and she looks over at me, frowning, "I don't know what we're going to do with her."

"I'm going to pile her shit every day until she learns to keep it clean."

"That won't solve anything."

"No, but I feel better."

One thing is she's in this with me. She knows we got a problem. We'll stand together on this. Neither kid ever got the better of us playing one against the other.

When the girl comes in somewhere after midnight, I'm still staring at the lily fields on the back of my eyelids, sawing logs, but she's out of bed like a shot and throws open the bedroom door, bangs it to bring down the walls. The girl is standing there in the hallway light weaving a little, drunk, I'd put money on it.

Out of her bedroom comes the vase, and she's sticking it under the girl's nose like she wants her to sniff it, take a long pull on it.

"What's this? Did you pee in here?"

"Ma!"

"Did you pee in here? Are you too lazy to go to the bathroom that you have to pee in a vase and let it stagnate on your vanity like your personal urinal? You live like a goat. I'm not going to put up with filth like this in the house. And I don't have to tell you what you're doing to your father."

She whaps the door with her arm and the girl sees the state of her boudoir and lets out a little cry of protest, the faucet starts running.

"See that room. You upset your father so much with this mess, look what he had to do. *Just to find his screwdriver*. He'll be upset for a week because of you. You think I'm going to let you get away with upsetting him like this, think again. You think he'll be able to get through a day of work, making him feel the way he does, think he'll be able to eat, when you do something like this to him?"

She shoves her shoulder, punches her in the room, and the girl stumbles against the doorframe. Drunk as a sailor. Sobbing.

"You get in there and make a nest for yourself like a goat. Pig! Drunk!" and slams her in the room, and comes back into the bedroom and lays down next to me.

"I don't know what we're going to do."

"We're doing all we can, honey, everything we can under the circumstances."

"We tried to teach her."

"You can lead a horse to water."

"I don't know what we would do any different," she says, and rests her head square in the middle of the pillow and I can see a deep cut between her brows, worried sick from what the girl's doing to her.

Bad blood, I want to say. It got handed down to her and it's running in her veins, and no matter how you cut it, we're not responsible for that. I wish I could do like the prayer plate she's got hanging on the bedroom wall, says, *ACCEPT THE THINGS WE CANNOT CHANGE*, but you got to be de-balled not to do something about that mess, because not doing anything, you can be held responsible for that, too.

BROTHER:

They're at her again. Like before she went in the Service. I don't what to do. Set the house on fire? Set their bed on fire, watch them wiggle in the flames? They'll run out of the bedroom with their heads blazing and all the wind in their screams won't put out the flames. My head is in flames. All this. I can't stand all this. Before she went in Service what they did was horrible. Now this. Last night I dreamt she crept upstairs, sat next to the bed and whispered, "You've got to do something, Mark, they're going to kill me." So real, so sweet with alcohol, I don't know if she really came up here or if she didn't. That's the kind of dream it was. So real that it actually happened, and wasn't a dream at all, and so awful that I turned it into a dream when I fell back to sleep.

She didn't come up here last night.

Couldn't have.

She couldn't have come out of her bedroom last night after the wicked witch nailed her door shut. I heard chains pulled across. Furniture pushed in place. Dungeon doors resounded in my head so my temples are about to explode.

Why don't they do it to me instead? I can take it better than she can. She's frail. The constant battering ditches her in. She has a thousand dents on the inside, she can't handle more. She's getting wrecked and soon nothing inside will work, she'll rust, parts will fall off. Stupid, stupid, stupid. She's no machine. She's soft and easily harmed, and they're slicing her. She'll scar and cripple. Why are they doing this? Why are we chained to this house? Why isn't there a separate door for dogs and children, I promise we'll come and go quietly, never ask for anything, be silent when we go, silent when we come home. Feed us downstairs, like you promised, Father. "You eat like pigs, we ought to slop you down in a basement trough." You can pet us like animals and yell at us to be silent and we will, shivering as we disappear into the hole your shouts open, hearing it slam shut behind us.

Why don't they choose me? At least I have a fighting chance. I can run. I've got a hard head that can take cuffs and a butt that welcomes the boot. They've chosen her to sacrifice when the most exalted sacrifice is the son. Shouldn't the son be held down on the altar? Why do they leave a witness at all? Isn't the smart thing to put out my eyes, puncture my eardrums, separate tongue from mouth? Yet I am unscathed. And I'm not sure I'm not glad. I am afraid I am the brother who pleads with the jury to hang him, but please spare his sister, who begs to bear the noose himself, but the moment both face the hangman, he would yell, "Take her first," pointing at his beloved sister. Perhaps it is all pose, as frightened as I am watching them flay the skin from her back, at the crucial moment, the instant I could save her, I would refuse to remove my shirt. Or maybe no one can stand in for her. Maybe she is the necessary sacrifice, ordained by a God I am too feeble to understand.

MOTHER:

It could have been such a perfect Saturday. Sun shining. Birds. I spent it cleaning, getting the house in order, moved chairs, vacuumed, got laundry caught up, took meatloaf down for dinner. There was a song in my heart. When I dusted the china cabinet, all the hand-painted dishes I had, flowers growing up the sides of them and bluejays around the middle, or the robins she painted on branches with their happy red breasts, I decided to wash them, too, and it made me happy running the cloth over them. A perfect Saturday, as perfect as they come. I was thinking of handwashing the doilies my mother crocheted, for the fun of it, feeling my fingers catch in the little white knots of thread, thinking it was a perfect Saturday, could have been. Guy was alongside the house running the hose over the Ford, radio propped in the window, listening to the news and it didn't sound like anything much was going on in the world that was going to bother Saturday. Pipes running in the floor. Sound of busyness. I listened to him talking to that woman next door, who for once wasn't complaining about her husband or son, and since there was a fence between him and her I knew she'd have a hard time draping herself on him. By the garage Mark was throwing the basketball through the hoop. Perfect. The ball bouncing, radio, suds hitting the sidedrive. I was singing at the top of my lungs and didn't even realize it until I heard her next door say, "She has a beautiful voice," and that made me feel good, too, even though it came from a foul-mouthed barfly. It made me remember when the kids were little and I'd sing out the window while I did dishes. Neighborhood children would sit in the empty lot next door so they could listen to me. Those days. Perfect Saturdays. Too bad my daughter didn't inherit my good disposition, she'd be a lot happier. She has her father's bad temper and wakes up with a mean look on her face in the morning like him. Mark's got my disposition. Me and him are the happy-go-lucky ones in the family.

Things roll off our backs, like ducks, the hard times roll off and we get on, a smile on our faces. He likes to sing, too. We got him a guitar when he got out of eighth grade that he likes to bang on upstairs, if he doesn't do it loud, it's not bad. But nobody will ever praise his voice. So what. He has a happy disposition. Doesn't seem to notice, goes along his happy way just like me.

These other two. You can see them bubbling inside every time any little thing happens. So sometimes we lose our tempers, it happens to me, but you have to put these things behind you. If you keep brooding about every little thing, you wind up with an ulcer. That's where she's headed. She still hasn't forgotten Thursday night and I want to say, like you say to little children when they cross their eyes, "Don't do that with your face. It'll get stuck that way and then what?" Downturned mouth and squinched eyes and then I don't care what kind of mini-skirt you wear, who's going to take you out then? Because I don't care, a plastic surgeon can't carve a frown off your face, he can cut and paste till you don't look like yourself, but a frown, that's a problem that starts in your heart, you've got to take care of it there before it'll go away. That's good advice that neither one of them wants to take. I'm telling you if they'd listen to me, I could get everything running right.

It's the first Saturday of the month. The air raid sirens just went off, so one o'clock. And she still hasn't come out of her room. I don't know how she can stay huddled in there with so many happy sounds going on in the house. She's surrounded by cheeriness and can't still be sleeping. It would take somebody deaf and dumb and blind to sleep through all these happy sounds. I think she's holding a grudge. She won't let go. Last night Guy went downstairs to putter around his workbench, making something out of two-by-fours and whatnot and she wasn't home from work yet, not that she ever comes straight home from work on Friday. Or any other night, for that matter. So I took a big plastic bag and went in there to help her out with her room. I felt a little bad about the way Guy tore it up the night before and I thought I'd go in there and find out what she had that she didn't need and get it straightened out for her. That way she wouldn't have to do it when she came home and everything would go a lot smoother because no telling when she'd come home.

This is the sort of thing I try to do around here when we hit a rough spot, make a cushion out of myself between her and him. I've always tried to intervene so that we can be one happy family. I believe that's what a mother is for.

She'd pushed her mattress back on the box springs, but that's all she'd done. It looked like a hurricane had hit in there, but that wasn't really so different from the way it looked before Guy went in there and had a conniption fit. There was everything everywhere. A shambles. But it was easy to see what had to be done so I dug in and started sifting. It wasn't too difficult to fill the first bag. Kleenex, old newspapers she'd carted in there and some old faded jeans, torn in the knee that were too damn tight on her anyway, filled that bag right up. Nothing she'd miss, that's for sure. A lot of the bottles and jars were empty. There were caps that didn't go with anything and old greeting cards from boy friends and high school friends and letters from guys that had shipped away from the base she was stationed on. Old stuff that was taking up room. It's a small room to begin with, it's no wonder she couldn't keep it clean all that stuff packed in there. Full of the sort of things a young girl would have trouble deciphering what's important and what's not. She had her discharge papers stuffed in a trashy book, marking the pages where they could get nothing but tattered and dirty. So I got rid of the book and folded the papers neatly and tucked them in the bottom of the first vanity drawer. Already I was making a difference. You could see how much easier it was going to be for her to keep it straight. I shoveled all the clothes he'd thrown on the floor with the ones she'd left hanging half off hangers in the closet and on the closet floor into a big pile at the foot of the bed and then went about sorting what still looked good on her, what was bright and cheerful from the dark, morose colors she collected when she was away, threw out all the too tight, too short or too low cut clothes that a mother knows get a young girl in trouble. It cut her closet right down so there was plenty of room to hang everything. There were shoes that had to go. Worn out. Scraped up beyond repair.

There were three vases in the room with old flowers in them. Three. No wonder she couldn't keep the water fresh. I threw out all the flowers and put the vases in the kitchen sink to be washed. Piled the curtains into the washer and while they were cleaning up, stripped the bed and threw out the old patch quilt she'd had on that bed since she was little. It had threads hanging off it everywhere and the colors were so faded that I was embarrassed to have her using it anymore. I put down a new K-Mart blanket I'd been saving. I swear, "Thoroughness" is my middle name. A couple of drawers in the vanity, and the bottom drawer of her dresser were still in place and I figured there was more than enough in them to justify sorting, so I emptied them on the dwindling pile of crap in the middle of the floor. There were old movie stubs, little plastic prizes she must have picked up at some school fair or other, six small stuffed animals that had collected so much dust I thought she must have used them for cleaning. She'd clearly outgrown these but hadn't gotten around to throwing them out. So I saved her the trouble. I put all her drawers in order. Got rid of the lipsticks she had that didn't suit her skin color, and believe me, after beauty school I know which ones are doing her a favor and which ones aren't. I polished the wood and vacuumed under the bed. And so I can't understand how it backfired.

She got home early last night, but it was after we went to bed. I was still laying there awake, pretty satisfied with myself and excited for her to find what I'd done for her. Guy was already rolled over, dead to the world. I don't think she was drinking because she made more noise than she usually does. She wasn't creeping in like an alley cat. She clicked on the light in her room, a line of light shot around the edges of our door, and she let out a cry, almost shouted, "What have you done?" It wasn't loud enough to wake Guy but it was almost a shout, which there is no excuse for when he's finally got a day off the next day and deserves his rest. And so do I.

"What have you done? Where's my letters? My clothes? Where's my yearbook?" The sobbing started. But she was also throwing things around. I got up to put a stop to that.

I walked in on her as she was tearing through the clothes in her closet, accusing me of what I don't know, "You did this, you did this, you did this," and not making sense and then she turned on me with tears running down her cheeks and said, "You threw out my yearbook, where's my yearbook," working herself into hysteria, as if her yearbook was that important. She hasn't looked at it in years. "I want my yearbook, I want my yearbook," the way she used to sob, "I want my mother, I want my mother, I want my mother," when other kids on the block would make fun of her teeth.

"Honey, it's upstairs on the bookshelf. I put it where it belongs."

"I want my yearbook."

Then she threw her shoe on the floor.

I'd had about enough out of her.

"You did this to me, you always do this to me."

"I didn't do anything but try to dig through some of the filth in here. You seem to like filth."

"I do like it. I do like it. I want my filthy room. I want my filthy room, goddamn it, goddamn it."

And, well, that told the whole story right there. Guy is always going on about how she came down the wrong side of the family blood. He says she's naturally lazy and sloppy, but I never expected her to come right out and admit it. She got on her feet, looking like she was going to hit me, I'd never seen her like that, walking toward me.

"Get out, get out of my room. I don't want you in this room ever. This is *my* room. I want you out."

She pushed the door closed in my face. I couldn't believe this is the thanks I get. She forgets the one that tore the whole place up, and then yells at her mother who was helping her put it back together again. And she doesn't realize she's only got one mother. And I'm not going to be here forever. She'll be sorry when I go but it won't do her any good then, regrets won't count for anything when I'm gone. I could go into my sewing machine right now and get scissors and slash my wrists and watch how she'd feel. One mother isn't very many when you treat her like she does. And I'm going to make a point of telling her so.

The minute she comes out of that bedroom.

Sister:

I earned a hundred and thirty-two dollars the other day. Wonder what Dad would think of that, think that makes me more important than him? I don't think he'd think that. I didn't exactly earn it. It fell out of the sky into my lap. That's a joke. Fell in my lap. And I put in twenty minutes. Not twenty years. Everything works out. This guy I met at the Cadieux Cafe played on my team on the hockey machine, kept nudging me by accident. It got funny, the way he'd turn sideways against me, by accident, he said, and before you know it, we were dancing slow, so close to the speakers we couldn't talk. We were up against each other and the bump-that-tells-it-all started, and I almost laughed in his face, bumping me like that, it's a joke without words I hear every time I turn around. There's nothing special about a guy's dick. Excuse my French.

And one thing led to another. We left together and walked out to our cars. I told him I'd follow him, but he said, no, he'd drive me back here to my car later, so we jumped into his car. A Jaguar. This guy was loaded and not just with booze. I took a closer look at his clothes and realized he was casual, but expensive. He had money coming out his ears. So. It didn't matter. Things took their course, at his house, but the problem was, he said, that he couldn't see me again, because his wife was coming back from a trip tomorrow and it wouldn't do to have the bed overcrowded. I got mad. Wish he'd told me sooner. And I told him so.

"What do you mean, wife? What are you doing in that bar anyway with a wife?"

"Man needs recreation," he said, "Sometimes a foray in the forest, a romp in the meadow."

"A romp in the meadow," for some reason dug in me and I looked at myself in his wife's mirror, and felt like a romp. That's all I was, a romp. A rump.

"You think I'm a tramp, don't you?" I said, "You think I jump in bed with anybody asks, don't you?"

And I felt worse all of the sudden than I'd felt in days, weeks. All the dirt came back again, of Jack, the fiasco with Tom, other guys. This guy sitting on the side of the bed with his arm around me might look good in his expensive clothes, but right there, right then, his belly was crumpled as cottage cheese and his toenails were yellow, unclipped, ragged. I felt like the lowest whore my father ever said I was. I got mad for crying, too. I pushed the heels of my hands in my eyes like I was trying to stop bleeding, stop an artery pumping out a crash victim, and everything I did made it worse.

I got tangled in my sweater when I was pulling it over my head and while I was wound up in it and could hardly move he put his hand on my stomach and I shrieked. What did he think he was doing? He was old enough to be my goddamn father and I didn't even see it until then, how old and flabby he was. But he kept on with his arm around me saying he thought I was okay. There was nothing wrong with me for being attracted to a man and then spending some time with him. Natural as anything on earth. And he started to stroke me again, but I held my own, and told him I couldn't, even if he turned out to be the nice guy I originally thought he was, because it felt like his wife was standing in the closet looking out at us because I noticed then a bra hanging on the door knob that I didn't see before and a lot of things that said he had a wife. "I don't know how I could be so stupid," I said, "I should have guessed."

He told me he would drive me back to my car, but I said I'd walk. He said he'd call me a cab, but he didn't want it pulling up in front of the house with the neighbors, so he said he'd tell them to pick me up on the corner of Kercheval so I only had two blocks to walk. Fine. Fine. And as I was leaving, he said, here's a couple of bucks for the cab and closed the door behind me. I was standing on the corner before I saw I was squeezing a hundred dollar bill in my hand. I got mad, but I got over it. It doesn't make me a whore. I didn't ask for anything and if he wants to feel better and give me something, that's his problem. Because I need money. I need money if I'm going to ever get a place of my own.

Getting out of there is A-Number-One priority.

If I had a place of my own I wouldn't have to wait around for the bars to close before I came home. I could stay in my place and read a book if I wanted to and I wouldn't have to depend on guys to take me places, any place that isn't home.

I think they're trying to get me out anyway.

They're either trying to force me out, or toilet train me. I can't figure out which. But I want out, out, out. As soon as I get the money.

I want to hate them from another house.

MOTHER:

"Honey, your Father and I have been talking it over and we think you're a little old to be living here."

"You can say that again."

"It hasn't been exactly smooth sailing since you got back."

"You're telling me."

"Simmer down, young lady."

"I'm listening."

"We feel there's enough friction and disruption to our life that we should try to correct things a little."

"I haven't got the money to move. I'm working on it, saving as much as I can. I want to get a place of my own. But I don't have the money for it yet."

"Who said anything about moving?"

"I thought you were throwing me out. You said you didn't want me living here. I'm saving as fast as I can."

"You giving money to the bartender to save for you? That how you're saving?"

"Guy, let's talk about this reasonably."

"Can't reason with a jackass."

"Guy! Now, honey, obviously, if a person gets too comfortable there's really no incentive for that person to do anything different, right? If a person's always got his meals handed to him, why cook his own? If his rent's paid, why move where it'll cost, right?"

"Uh, huh."

"Well, then you agree. You see our point."

"I think so."

"Good."

"You don't want me to stay here. You want me out on my own."

"No, honey, how do you get these things in your head? Stay as long as you need while you're getting ready to have a place of your own. In my day, a girl stayed home until she got married and you can stay here till you get married if you want to."

"God help us."

"Guy, shut up. This is your home, and you've got a room and food and we'll be here for you any time you need us."

"Then why are you telling me to get out?"

"We're not. We only want to provide a little incentive for you to take control of your life. A little responsibility. Everybody's got to make a contribution to the world. If you're not putting in, you're taking away. And you don't want to be a taker, do you? That's all we're saying. You know what I'm saying?"

"Everybody's got to do something."

"Exactly. So you won't mind making a contribution around here. It's fair. And it's the only way to learn responsibility. And in the long run we think you'll feel better about yourself."

"Dust, do dishes, what?"

"Your mother means from now on you pay rent."

"Rent, Jesus Christ!"

"Cash on the barrelhead."

"How can I save money to get my own place if I have to pay rent around here?"

"Now don't get excited, honey, it's not much."

"How much?"

"We just want you to contribute a little something for living expenses. It'll get you more in the swing of how the world runs."

"Fifty bucks a week."

"That's less than half what you make. You can save the other half."

"How can I get out? What can I do? Sit around here all the time? I'm trapped! You're trapping me!"

"Well, it wouldn't hurt you to sit home and read a book once in a while. And there's always food in the refrigerator."

"I don't want to sit around here and eat Velveeta sandwiches."

"You don't like it, kiddo, there's the door. Don't let it catch your ass on the way out."

"What's wrong with Velveeta?"

Father:

I was born under a dark cloud. There's one thing you got to do with a dark cloud looming over you, keep your mouth shut. Otherwise, you look up, you drown. Oh, you get wet either way. You can't help that. That's the way it is. But maybe, just maybe you won't drown. I am not lucky. I never been lucky. I don't depend on luck. I do my work and stay out from underfoot. But I got this problem and it's especially bad when you're born like I said, under a cloud, that's I don't keep my mouth shut. I got something to say, I know I should keep it inside, that's the prudent thing, but before the thought that says, "Bite your tongue" gets through, I already said what I had to say. There it is and I take the consequences. Lost a tooth that way. Busted my wrist that way. Once took a piece of pipe on the bridge of my nose. But still, I got something to say, I say it. There it is. Goddamn it. I don't regret it. For a working stiff the one gold on this earth is nobody owns your thoughts, and truth be told, that gold's worth nothing unless I spend it the way I want to.

That's why I stayed a working stiff. I could have moved up. They wanted me to become a supervisor half dozen times through the years, but I wasn't going to step out of the union, not with that dark cloud and my mouth. I'd been on my ass long ago. I see bosses shiver and eat shit, trying to make like it tastes good, because they forgot what they were born to do. Work. Do the job. Pick up a shovel.

I traded one bunch of headaches for another when I moved off the poles and out of the sewers indoors, on the main relays. It meant I had a boss at my elbow telling me how to go about my job. I'd tell them go over to the corner and stick one thumb in their ass and one thumb in their mouth and for a good time, every once in a while, switch. I'd call them when I got whatever job done and they could tell me if I tied the wires pretty, or did it fast enough.

They didn't like it, they could write me up. That's what we got an arbitration board for, I'd say, so when some dumb fuck in a tie thinks for a second he knows more than the man doing the job, we can put a whole room full of people together to tell him how dumb he is. I did my job good all these years. I got wrote up not very often, and the bosses learned to leave me alone, let me work.

The job is climbing, just like the poles, only up ladders, up and down walls of wire that hum and click in like crazy as power surges through. They give you a work order, you climb the ladder and adjust. It's not simple, but I never had a college education either. Just enough brains to get laid when my dick's pointing to heaven and to piss when it's pointing to hell. That's more knowledge than these sorry bastards in ties. I get along from year to year. New boss comes in the building he always throws his weight around, pretends he can actually find his dick in a dark room. He scrambles like a chimpanzee, do this do that, a couple of weeks everybody only does what he says, that way everything gets thoroughly fucked up, orders fall behind. We got customers beating on the doors and windows to turn on the power and this guy gets heat from his boss, and when he's shivering and fretting for his job, we say we can get everything running fine if he goes over in the corner and does exactly what we tell him to do with his thumbs. Things settle down and we keep going. Day after day. Year after year.

Twenty years I been doing this. You'd think I know how not to let the white shirt bastards get to me. But one finally did. I think it's the problem with the girl that's had me tense. I'm not getting sleep I need. I'm ready to jump down anybody's throat. Still, twenty years.

This guy, not one of the guys who came up through the ranks, but this fat bastard been in my face for years, doesn't like my attitude, as if they bought my attitude when they give me the job. Never been in the field. Never climbed a pole. Never went down a sewer after a line. Never went into a slum house with felons screwing on the bed in the next room while you're tying down a fuse box. Got a wad of chewing gum going in his teeth and all the while he's bumping my elbow and shoving a finger in my job to show me how wrong I'm doing it.

His name is Garvey. We call him "Gravy," or "Mashed

Potatoes," short for "Mashed Potatoes and Gravy," and short for when he's not stuffing his yap, he's using it to mash up any job we got going. Insists on cross-tying, double running circuits, says if we don't wear rubber gloves on certain circuits, he'll write us up. When it comes to safety regulations, he knows he's got us, because it's one area the union can't back us up. Mainly he knows how to waste our time and get away with it. Twenty years I know what wire is going to knock me on my ass if I poke it. But he's strictly training manual, and even that's not so bad, but it's his way of going about it.

"Well, well, well, what have we here?"

He holds up the end of a live wire clipped in a high tension snare.

"This could make some poor fellow's hair stand up. And it's just hanging here."

"I got it, Gravy, leave it alone."

"But, but, but, but," his voice rising like he's singing, "My dear man . . ."

He knows this faggot voice gets me.

"Anybody can walk by here and get his ear burned. Would you want to burn someone's ear, my dear man?"

I take the wire away from him and tie it down. Now he holds a fist full of work orders in front of me, says, "Sir, I can't read your writing on these orders. They're marked done, but what exactly is done, what's this chicken scratch mean? You replaced a couple of resistors, or the whole unit? I think you better rewrite these orders, my dear man, sir."

"You know I put in the whole fucking unit. You were standing right here."

"Well, well, well, well, I know that. And you know that. Yes, yesssss, we know. But in six months will we know? Will I remember? Will you? Not in your life. And this gibberish will not help at all."

"Who's going to look at a work order again, Gravy? Nobody. It works. When it don't work, we'll fix it again."

He looks both ways up and down the frame to see if anybody can hear us, then steps two rungs up the ladder so his face is in mine, and says, "My dear sir, you are such a unabated masturbated fucker I'm going to make you rewrite every one of these, and you'll get this job done today, too, and I'll write your ass up if you don't finish both of them, you lazy prick."

Normally I would have laughed it off, told him to jack off in his baloney sandwich, but when he called me lazy and a picture of the girl jumped in my mind, it flipped my switch, like in the Marines, time a jack-off came up behind me when I was getting ready to hit the beach. I had my hands in my pockets and the asshole grabbed my wrists and pulled down. Both my pockets tore and he thought it was the funniest thing since Chaplin ate a shoe, but I turned and grabbed him by the throat with one hand and the fingernails of the other tore my back to ribbons clawing to get the knife that, fortunately for his ass, I'd left in my locker because I was going shore side. He knew I was going for my knife, too. He knew if I'd had it, I'd have gutted him, right there. He felt it. I wasn't thinking. I was doing. I had scabs on my back for three weeks.

When Gravy said that, he fanned the work orders over my nose a couple of times and stepped back down to the floor. Any other time I'd have ignored him, maybe farted in his face, his nose was at the right height to really make an impression, but I looked at him a second and how he called me lazy, swishing those papers in my face . . .

Next thing I had a good sized crescent wrench in my hand and I clipped him across the side of the jaw, didn't feel too hard, hard enough I guess, one easy swing, plenty of follow through, and the left side of his jaw popped at a funny angle and he hit the deck.

Easy to see he tripped getting off the ladder. Far as I was concerned. My word against his. I looked at him on the rubber mat and turned back to finish the job I was doing. Others saw it different. His boss and his boss's boss were at the end of the aisle watching, and they came running.

That's how I lost my job.

Twenty years and it went away.

MOTHER:

He got up on time and I heard him banging his comb on the sink. He knows that irritates me, but he's done it every day since we got married. The kettle was whistling in the kitchen, our places were set, vitamin pills under the overturned juice glasses so they wouldn't roll off the table. There was a box of cornflakes for me and Wheaties for him in front of our bowls and oatmeal for the boy set up by the stove. He was hacking and spitting like he always does, and he came out of the bathroom in the creased pants he wears for work. He ate his toast, hooking it around the newspaper and I read the funnies while he read the sports and the front page and Mark came downstairs right on time and started banging the sauce pan around with the oatmeal in it. After breakfast, he slipped into the bathroom to clean his partial and then he came out of there right on time, picked up the car keys and shot out the back door, a couple of minutes ahead of me, like he always does, to pull my car down the sidedrive because he's afraid that I'm going to take the gutter drain pipe off the side of the house because I don't back up as good as he does. But I haven't done it yet. And I'm a better driver than he gives me credit for. He came in, shaved, combed, wearing one of his work shirts with the sleeves rolled up, like he always does, and he pulled open the door on the front of the end table and put his wallet in his pocket, his lighter, his pocket knife that I'm always afraid is going to open up and cut him where it hurts, and while I was pulling on my jacket and putting my lipstick in my purse, he did something different. He reached under the lampshade and switched on the light. He took a whole carton of cigarettes from under the table and put it next to his ashtray. Then he took out his magazine and sat down and folded one leg over the other and lit a cigarette. It jarred me. Until then everything felt all right. But everything was changed. He didn't say anything, he didn't get up and kiss me goodbye, which he usually does.

I picked up my purse and left.

When I got home he was sitting there like he always does, already changed from his work clothes into his flannel shirt and dungarees, waiting for me to get dinner started, reading *The Rise and Fall of the Third Reich*, like nothing had changed, but I could see there was only one unopened pack of cigarettes in the carton, the ashtray was overflowing and another ashtray from my end table was sitting next to his, that one overflowing, too, and the ashes moving around the table top when I closed the door and the wind pushed them this way and that. It's like everything all at once had frothed over and was coming out of a hole in the middle of that ashtray, ashes coming up, spilling out, like a hole we'd been incinerating things in suddenly exploded in our faces.

"Hello," I sang out, to let Mark upstairs know I was home and to start him washing up for supper. And to be cheerful.

He scowled at me and adjusted his leg over the arm of the chair and went on reading. He was in a foul mood, sure, not feeling good, but what was I supposed to do? I didn't feel good either. And I'm the one that worked all day. Earning my measly fifty dollars more than he earned that day.

I started the electric fry pan going and put in the roast beef and potatoes left from Sunday.

When he sat down to eat he didn't say anything, but that wasn't unusual. We don't bother with talk most of the time when we eat. We're not there to chitchat. But he pulled his chair out, scraping it across the linoleum in an especially long drawn out scrape that set my nerves vibrating, and I said, "Guy, do you have to do that?"

He looked at me and then looked down at his plate and started eating.

I said, "You don't have to do that, you know. This floor costs money."

"I paid for the floor, I'll scrape the floor."

Well, the floor isn't paid for, I wanted to say. We still have a mortgage. But I didn't. Because I know he'd say his This-is-my-house speech that I've heard just about enough, like when he got the girl going, because she was so outraged at her Uncle Eli's running around and how it made my sister feel.

"He's got a wife and he's got no right to do that right under her nose."

"Why not?"

"Because he's married."

"He brings home a paycheck, don't he? She brings in nothing. He works every day, she sits on her ass. He can do anything he wants. He earned the right. He wants to chase tail, he's got the right. He wants to blow his money on that fat Buick, he's got the right. She wants to complain about it, he can give her the back of his hand as far as I'm concerned."

"Sure. He can beat her if he wants to."

"Absolutely. Long as he brings in the bacon, he's got the right. I got no judgement to make on him."

"Don't be ridiculous, Guy." I can't stand it when he makes stupid remarks like that.

"Nobody has the right to beat another human being. Nobody, nobody, nobody can beat another person like they're a child or a dog."

"Far as I'm concerned he's got every right. Man's got only one obligation. That's to feed his family. He does that, every day of his life I don't care how drunk he got the night before or how many pieces of tail he knocked off, he gets up and goes to work. He's got the right."

Well, he doesn't have the right to scrape my linoleum, and I could smack him for it.

FATHER:

I don't regret hitting him. Not in your life. I'd hit him again. I'd hit him harder. I'd take his head off if I could get a good swing. I'm sorry I missed his teeth. Son of a bitch had it coming. They think because they give you a job you're supposed to take any shit they hand out. "Ah," they say, "You don't have to take our shit, only if you want the job." As if a working stiff doesn't have a right to a job. Simple as that. Like they're doing us a favor giving us work, when in fact, there wouldn't even be electric power if there weren't a hundred thousand working stiffs doing the work. They don't do it. They direct. They manage. They think out the Big Picture. And they think this makes them holier than the stiff tying down the wires. Well, it don't. "If you want the job, if you want to work for us, you're going to have to swallow your dignity, that's one lump of spit that'll get you in trouble if it hits our floor, no you swallow that, and you be a good dog and do what we say, and in the way we say you got to do it, and smile, you lowly bastard, while you're doing it." But everybody has their limit, beyond this line a man does not go. I guess my limit is twenty years. I been eating shit till I could grow corn on my tongue.

They want me to thank them for the job. They should thank me for doing it.

I should have tore out his jawbone and used it to smash all three of them.

So what do I got to do, apologize to my family? Tell them I'm sorry I lost my temper? I couldn't be happier. It might be the best day's work I ever did, rolling that wrench through the air, tapping that scummy ass wipe. And I don't care the eye she's putting on me, when she's putting on her coat to go to work like she's putting on my balls, too, and I can hear them clanking together as she walks out that door. I'm not putting up with that. That boy better get his ass off to school right now. I don't care it's time or not. It's time if I say it's time. And we'll see about the girl. There's goddamn money to goddamn make.

Jesus, twenty years, up in smoke.

Maybe I should have been a cop like Uncle Tony so some punk gets out of line I swat him across the back of the thighs with a nightstick and nobody thinks anything about it.

And I told her not to leave the want ads out for me because I can find them my own goddamn self, thank you, and she better listen to what I say. Twenty years. How can you lose twenty years fast like that? Doesn't twenty years count? I thought it might, but I was stupid. I'm a rotten fence post they yanked out and will never think about again. What am I going to do? As if there's another electric company. Can't go down the block, not like factory work, you go down the line to the next factory, keep pounding doors till someone lets you in. Am I going to be a forklift driver? A milkman? I'm electrical, but I'm not an electrician. I'm a skilled worker who's only got the skill to work one place, goddamn Edison, and it doesn't matter if I beg, if I walk my knees on broken glass all the way downtown, when they send a file to the basement, I been at the company long enough to know, it's lost for good. I got the skill and no place to use it. I might as well be a blacksmith. I started out with nothing and twenty years that's what I still got. In that light, I guess nothing is lost. Just living.

I noticed she circled the jobs her father held through the years. That yahoo. Where'd he get? He's been a bum since the doctor cut his cord. The only thing he's been able to hang on to is a can of beer. She's saying there's a lot of things I can do. There *is* a lot I can do, but there's no goddamn jobs to do anything on.

"Honey, now don't get mad, but there's something you haven't thought about, but there's a lot of guys getting into it now."

I'm open, I ain't too proud to do what I have to do to feed my family. "What?"

"You could go to beauty school."

I didn't tear her head off, I could have tore her head off. I could have tore her head off and used it to play volley ball, if I could have thought of anything that moment, I would have tore her head off, but I was so stunned I sat there and looked at her.

"See, you didn't think of that."

"Jesus, next thing I'll throw a Tupperware party."

"Now there's another idea!"

I started laughing and then I went downstairs and beat my knuckles bloody on the punching bag.

BROTHER:

They've chosen her hair.

Her lush, sexual plumage.

They've always aimed at it. I should have known they would go after it next. Eleven years old:

"Stop chewing your hair." It falls from her mouth, the ends wet, in a moment, it's in her mouth again. "Stop that."

Long, brown, lovely hair.

"These braids will catch in the spokes of your bicycle and break your neck. That's what happened to Isadora Duncan. She was a famous dancer and her head popped off."

To convince her to keep her hair short.

It growing profusely, though yanked with brush and comb, untamed, pouring out of her like wild vines, knotted, tangled, twisted.

"Sorry, honey, every woman goes through this with her hair. You'll have to get used to it."

Sudsing, digging.

"You're hurting me."

Pulling her hair as if she's fighting with her, how women fight, with hair. The old lady kicked her ass twice a week.

And then she grew up. Nobody touched her hair. She washed it and ran the comb down the length of it, a hundred times, it glistened, crackled with static. Long enough to let down from her window. And she did. She did. My sister, Rapunzel, weaving breath-taking threads through her comb. She slept on huge rollers at night, with plastic needles poking her skull. To be beautiful. She washed it with three kinds of shampoo and four conditioners, the matting fell away. She let it grow to her shoulders, her back, beyond. Sometimes she teased it high, like a huge cake, sprayed a whole can of AquaNet on it to hold it solid against wind. Her most spectacular ornament. Now she wears it long, ratted, with a flip at the shoulders, lovely, she cares for nothing better.

"When are you going to wash your hair?"

"I washed it. I wash it every day."

"It doesn't look like it. It looks like something's growing in there. Something could nest. Why don't you cut your hair like a grownup."

The old lady wants her to cut and coil her hair in tight ringlets like springs. She'd be satisfied if she could trim it like a hedge, in a neat box, or carefully controlled curves, fix it with a coat of shellack so it wouldn't even dent if a gang of angry hair mashers attack it with hammers. She doesn't think it's too much to ask. What's the big deal? She can look like every girl on the street, or have some individuality. She'd prefer her to look like every girl of twenty years ago, when girls knew how to make themselves look good. Not this ugly ratting, piling, stringy, falls of hair on top of disgusting miniskirt cut so high up, "You can practically see more than any decent person would want to see," that more personal hair.

But the old lady's wish was not enough to make it happen. It was him. It was him looking at her miniskirt that made her hair come off. I should have stayed upstairs, should have kept the stereo loud, I wouldn't have heard and I never would have seen, but I went downstairs like I wanted to get a glass of water and I heard and I saw.

"You can't tell me when to come home."

"We sure as hell can. And we goddamn will."

"What are you doing out there?"

"It's none of your business."

"Child of mine, anything you do is my business, and don't you forget it."

"What are you doing out there till all hours?"

"Nothing. Talking."

"You sure do a lot of talking out there for someone we don't hear anything out of. What do you have to say that's so important you have to stay out till all hours to say it. If it's so important maybe you should talk to your parents about it. We can help you with these important matters. C'mon, let's hear what's so important."

"It's not so important."

"Oh, you stay out till goddamn dawn talking about things that aren't important. That's a good goddamn reason to not get up in the morning, because let me tell you, missy, getting your ass into work *is* important, and if you don't think so then we better talk about that right now."

"You're twisting my words."

"So you're not out there talking, what do you do?"

"Nothing."

"You're there, nobody talks, nobody gets up walks across the room, quiet, clock's ticking, till it's goddamn dawn and then you come traipsing back here. Think you'd want to say something here if nobody talks when you're out."

"There's talk."

"Well, I want to know one thing, you got to solve a little mystery for me, what I want you to clear up is this question, when you do this talking, are you standing, sitting or on your back?"

"Guy."

"I talk how I want to when I'm out of here."

"Well, it's got to be pretty interesting talk for you to get all dolled up like a whore to do it."

"I don't dress like a whore."

"Oh? That's why you got the crack of your ass hanging out? Why don't you hang a price tag on your butt? Then nobody's got to ask, and that's a little less talk you got to be bothered with."

"He's right. Your dresses are too damn short."

"They're not short. It's how everybody wears them and I don't care what you think. I think you're stupid."

"You think I'm stupid? You think I'm stupid I say something my girl's on the street advertising like a billboard."

"Don't you ever call, don't you ever call your father stupid. You don't ever, ever call your father stupid."

I was standing in the hallway, where I'm nothing, where I watch and nobody sees me. The old man comes off his chair, a bullet past me into the bathroom, comes out with a towel in his fist.

"I'll tell you what you're gonna do. I'll tell you and then you'll know what you're gonna do."

The old lady is shaking her arm, like she's five years old and she's trying to pull her arm away, but no good, she swings around at the end of the old lady's claws, wagging side to side.

"Don't you ever, ever . . ."

"You're gonna do this, you walk through this living room, you're gonna wear a goddamn towel over your naked ass because I'm tired of you parading through a decent home like you're out on the street, something," he throws the towel and it wraps around her face, "Tuck it in."

The old lady pulls down the towel and begins to push it in her skirt, practically pushing the miniskirt right off her hips. She's got a look on her face as the old lady does this like realization she's standing in a bath of acid, and the old lady picks up where the old man leaves off like his voice somehow leaped out of his throat into hers, "From now on you're going to keep your butt covered around here, you're not going to slink through here in front of your parents with your legs uncovered all the way up to your crotch. Do you want people to see your crotch? Do you think that's pretty? Well, I have news for you, nobody wants to see up your crotch because it's so disgusting it turns my stomach. And you're not going to have your hair sticking out like a banshee, no, you're going to look like a young lady when you go through this living room, because that's how we brought you up. Look at this. Look at this." The old lady grabs her hair, "It's a rat's nest. Rodents live in here. Vermin. You don't know what's hatching in your hair because you don't even wash it, you keep your filthy hair behind you and don't even look in a mirror because you're afraid of what you're going to find crawling around in it, aren't you, aren't you? Well, not anymore." The old lady drags her backwards into the kitchen by the hair, and she tries to grab at the hands that are tearing at her, but can't find them.

The old man says, "You put your hands down by your sides and sit still."

The old lady throws her into a kitchen chair and I haven't done anything, moved into the living room where I can see her in the chair, a scarecrow, a scared crow, pale, stricken look, and the old lady's face is mottled with red and she's pulled her hair razor out of the drawer and her hands whir like fans,

like a swarm of insects,

like a flood of rats,

like a sandstorm,

like a firestorm,
a propeller,
a switchblade,
rabid teeth,

hacking it off and flying off her fingers on the table and sink and floor.

"Sit still, young lady, and I'll make you look decent if it's possible, if it's the last thing I do, if I die today, you'll walk out that door you'll look decent at my goddamn funeral. Are you trying to kill me? Do you want to see your mother dead, is that it? You want to drive me into an early grave you're doing a pretty good job of it."

The hair falls off, and I don't do anything, can't do anything, nothing to do, but stand there.

Her face is still, and when the head jerks my way and eyes blink open, she doesn't see me, the face is dry, dry as stone, as sand, my mouth filling with salt, my cheeks burning, the room trembles and shivers and I want to run but am rooted to this spot. My feet buried in the rug won't budge, arms tied to sides, won't lift, if I could shut my eyes, shut them, can't.

"Get the hell out of here," the old man shoves me toward the upstairs door, "You're needed, we'll call you."

To my room and can't do anything. Still yelling downstairs, silence, and now sitting on the edge of the bed, I didn't do anything.

Her lush plumage.

So quiet, now this?

What happened? Why now?

□ □ □

From the first day he lost his job, he's been sinking into that chair, his back and legs spread into deep grooves. He's as brown as the upholstery. He's shriveling into it, the chair is a solution that's dissolving him. He says the same things, broken record, "Get a job," "Keep a job," "Eat shit," "This is my house," but he does it from deeper and deeper sunk in that chair. Will it swallow him? Is the chair a jaw closing over him? "Women are whores," "Detroit is a shithole," "Get an education," but in a voice that is somehow thinner, doesn't carry the same weight of authority, as if a wind blowing around him carries off the words, and it doesn't matter if I sit across the room, or lean over the chair with my ear next to his mouth, the substance of the words is evaporating so I can barely hear him.

And the smoke that blows around him.

All this because he lost his job?

I thought the old man was more than a job. A rock. The forgotten face on Mount Rushmore. He's always bellowed out from that chair. Even when he's speaking through gritted teeth in an angry mutter, his words have reached the furthest corners of the house. The glass jars in the fruit cellar tremble. The attic rafters take a hard thump. His voice has pushed the covers off my bed and curdled milk in the refrigerator. With a brief curse he's brought us all to our feet, dashing with boxes and pans, paper and cups, the necessary chore, whatever it is, sometimes demanded with less than a whisper, a glance loud as a shout that makes our shoes fill with sweat.

"I've got a bone to pick with you," is the phrase he spoke when I was out of line. He'd say it while we were driving down Connor. His hands never left the steering wheel except to bring the cigarette to his lips, his eyes never left the road, but whatever came next, he meant business and I was suddenly cramping with a desperate need to shit. Now that voice sunk inside him.

And I don't know if it's in hibernation or hiding, or if he's disappearing from the face of the earth, dying in a way I never expected, simply erasing, so that at the end of this process there will be nothing but yellow smoke stain left that coats the lampshades, makes books on the shelves upstairs sticky, weaves itself into our clothes, and his disappearance is more mysterious even than smoke. Without a job, it's as if he is consuming himself, gnawing his own limbs until there is nothing left but the hole where his mouth was.

The dark cloud he's always talking about has lowered. He's shadow. And he goes to bed early, earlier than ever. She does, too. She seems tired. Not him. But they're both gone before the evening begins.

And then he gets up later, and doesn't seem rested at all.

Now this.

SISTER:

I'm nothing without hair.
I'm nothing without hair.
Don't look at me.
Please don't look.
I can't cover my head all the time.
Don't look. Please.
I don't want anybody to look at me.
Ignore me.
Hair's gone.
I'm nothing.
Got nothing.
What's happened.
Nothing.
Because only nothing can happen to nothing.
I'm nothing.
Nothing happened.

FATHER:

Stop bellyaching. It'll grow.

CHAPTER

FOUR

OLD

HENRY

MOTHER:

It's what happens from sitting around too much. Energy builds up and you start twitching your arms and jiggling your legs like there's wires attached, or you're getting electric shocks. Twitching, jiggling. You can't sit still unless you get rid of that energy. I do vacuuming, and I go to work. That pretty much takes care of it. And cleaning. We go out to eat on Friday nights after work and that pretty well gets rid of excess energy I have left at the end of the week. It goes away like steam off a fried egg, cooling down by getting rid of that energy and I feel relaxed, like a cold, congealed egg, on Friday night. And then every other Saturday or so, because we have a very good sex life, we get rid of a little bit more energy, what's left by then isn't much, after all, we're in our forties, so the little bit we get rid of in bed feels fine. And Saturday is the best day for it, because after the house is in order, we have the whole day to rest and get ready for it. That's the right amount for us. Every other Saturday.

It's the foundation of a very good relationship to know how to be together like that and we've always had a very good foundation. Except those years when I was sick and then we pretty much blew off our excess energy in other ways. He built the room on the back of the house and I chased after the kids, or I'd lie down with a warm towel over my forehead. It didn't bother us much. We still had a very good relationship despite that we weren't practicing intercourse with each other those years. I was too sick and tired and he found a million and one things to keep him busy around the house. We didn't miss it. When the heart of your relationship is very good, what's to miss? It's only the icing on the cake. We didn't even talk about it. Which goes to show we had a very good marriage even during the tough years when it wasn't any good.

A good marriage comes from understanding how much to give

and how much to take and when the other person is tired. And our marriage has always been very, very good. He always knows when I'm tired. I'm not coy. I tell him. Believe me, it's not easy being a mother and a wife and having Saturday come around like clockwork every two weeks. But I've done pretty darn good. Very good.

I've made sure I haven't had too much energy building up inside me. It can make you blow. Think of it like a balloon when you put too much air in it. It blows up right in your face, bang, you're covered with saliva. A good marriage can turn into a mess if one person has more energy building up inside him than the other person. So you have to watch out. Balance. Balance is the key to a good marriage and we've been balanced right for each other all these years. And now this has happened.

Maybe the best thing for him right now is to take over the laundry. Running those stairs can really take it out of you. But with grown kids and him only in his "around the house" clothes these days, we're not getting enough clothes dirty to burn off that energy from him. And he can only cut the grass so many times a week. And we don't need another room on the back of the house. So that's out of the question.

I don't know.

It's out of balance.

I try to remind him that some of us have to WORK in the morning.

He's turning into a goat.

A randy goat.

A glutton for you-know-what.

The first week nothing happened. He sat in his chair and smoked cigarettes. He'd have dinner and then he'd go back to his chair and smoke until I went to bed. He'd sit up till two or three by himself, reading, and I'd hear the late, late movie droning through the walls. He folded in on himself like his clothes had nobody in them. Smoke coming out. He had a mean look on his face and I did my best to encourage him, tell him ways to help himself by looking through the newspaper, but I didn't keep that up because the meanness got worse, instead of better. If I was him, I'd appreciate some help. But father and daughter, two of a kind, you can't tell them anything. So it seemed better to simply leave the classifieds laying around on tables or by his footstool like I casually forgot it, rather than point it out to him. First week, okay, he needs time to catch his breath, okay, okay.

Second week Wednesday he puts his books down when I got up to brush my teeth and he started setting the breakfast table for morning, same schedule we were on all these years we both been working. He got ready for bed along with me and climbed in like always. So far so good. Only when I turned out the lights, he didn't roll over like he's supposed to. I was sleepy. I worked all day. I was tired. His hand started over my ribs and he moved next to me like it was Saturday and we just got married. I giggled, "Honey, it's a work night, you goat," and he chuckled his dirty chuckle, "So?" and he kept right on coming at me. House afire. It was so surprising I thought if I lost a half hour sleep, I could make it up a little bit tomorrow night, a little bit the next night, and then take an especially long nap Saturday afternoon, and I'd recover from it fine, so why not? I gave in. It was like throwing kerosene on a tiny, little match, because Thursday night he was right back there, bucking.

It was flattering at first, like being on a honeymoon, except, as I reminded him, I had to work in the morning, not like some people. But that didn't seem to cut any butter with him. He had too much energy built up from sitting around and if he didn't come at me, I thought he might blow up, so I tried to be a good sport, but you know it's not only the half hour, but you have to get up and clean yourself afterwards and of course change the sheets, so he was wearing me out. I tried going to bed right after the sitcoms, but he'd get ready then, too. Then before the sitcoms. Didn't work. Then a couple times I tried saying after supper dishes, "Well, I think I'll retire." He stretched, yawned, "Me, too."

I tried sneaking in there while he was downstairs putting throw rugs in the dryer, and I'd act dead when he rolled in later, but there was no stopping him. I pulled the afghan up around my neck and fell asleep in my chair, letting the book drop to the floor and he still didn't get the hint. He woke me up, said, "It's time, honey." The last stab finally saved me: I fell asleep on the bed with my clothes on and refused to wake up even when he was tickling my feet and shaking the covers to roll me around.

Too much energy. Boiling over.

SISTER:

They're robbing me blind. And they know it. They're trapping me. They *were* going to leave me a few crumbs. Now, nothing. I'll never get out of here. I'll be an old maid with wrinkles on my buns and stringy grey hair nobody wants to touch. I'll turn into a goofy spinster stuck in a nursing home that whops visitors with a cane to get attention. I'm wasting my life. And I can't go. They won't let me. I'd like to whop them with a cane. Him, I'd like to whop him. Stupid. Next thing they'll pawn the silverware in my hope chest. Sell my clothes. They want me here. They need me here. Now I'm the one bringing in the money. They want me. Because stupid lost his job. Because stupid had to hit somebody in the mouth and lose his job, they're taking everything away from me. I'll come out of the shower and discover they sold my skirts. "Here, go to work in a towel, fold it like this around you and nobody will know the difference. A terry cloth skirt! How marvelous! Beautiful! Gorgeous! Nobody will notice." That's what I'm afraid of, nobody will notice that I'm dressed like shit and I look like shit and they only let me have thirty dollars a week. Because stupid hit somebody in the mouth and they won't even give him unemployment. He has to pay a big fine. He should go to jail. At least then they'd feed him and I wouldn't have to.

"Honey, we're going to need a little more money to meet payments around here. Until your father gets something."

"How am I supposed to save to get my own place?"

"Well, actually, it makes more sense if you stay here for a few months. Until we get back on our feet."

"But I don't want to."

"You'd turn your back on your family? Is that the way we raised you, to forget the people that stayed by you? That's not how we do things in this family. That's not the kind of family we are, honey, we stick together. Thick and thin."

I don't want to stay. I want to get away from them, but I feel awful even thinking about it. I'm walking in mud, can't lift my shoes, they have me, mouth full of mud, I can't talk.

"You know we've always been there for you. You want us to lose this house that we worked all our lives to keep? They'll come and take the cars if we can't make payments. How would you feel if you saw someone out there stealing our car and when you asked them about it, they showed you a paper that says we lost it. They'll put our furniture at the curb, they'll throw us in the street."

"Who, who?"

"The bank, honey, because they don't care if we have to eat out of garbage cans, it's okay with them. Do you want to see us starve? You want to see your brother lose his education and start stealing like these kids you read about and me and your father and brother rummaging through garbage cans?"

"Where's your savings? What have you been doing all these years?"

"We live hand to mouth. All we have is what we make. We always thought when you kids grew up we'd start to lay a little bit aside. And with pension and social security, we'd be all right. Now this happens."

They want everything. I'll have to go to work in a barrel, or in clothes so old and raggedy and smelly they'll make me sit in a corner by myself. Because stupid lost his job.

He says, "You don't want to help. Fine. That's fine. Nobody's begging you. Keep your money. Buy dresses. Get your hair fixed. Perfume. Who cares about us? You go your merry way and do what you want to. We'll get by fine without your money. Who needs you?"

I want to say, "You need me, stupid, you need me and you need my money, and you better shut up or I'll light it on fire in your ashtray and you can shove the ashes up your ass and see how good my money spends then. Because I can do that if I want to because it's *my* money. I earned it. Not you. You can't even get a job because you beat up somebody and you're too old." I don't know what I could say if some company called for a recommendation. "I don't know," I'd have to say, "He gets violent, these whims where he says mean things. If you have anybody in your shop with any feelings, better not hire my father. No, not even for a janitor, because he'll say things that'll drive the customers away. He's a foul one. Is he honest? Sure, he's honest. He says what's on his mind even if it pisses off your boss' boss' boss' boss and the heat filters down on your head. Oh, you mean is he *honest* honest. Absolutely. Of course, he's robbing me blind, but that's none of your business. I shouldn't even mention it. It's strictly a family matter. You see in our family, it's perfectly all right to rob each other blind as long as we do it in the house. He'd never steal from a stranger. Just me." It'd be a tough recommendation, but I learned right from the stupid horse's mouth, say what's on your mind. Don't pull any punches. Well, I'm not, buster.

How can they do this to me?

I caught her in my room looking at a pay stub, making sure I don't hold out on them.

Thank God there are bars to go to after work. I can drink water until somebody buys me a highball.

I'm not about to come home. I hate coming home.

He's sitting here at two in the morning, three, four. I stay out as long as I can.

But he can sit there and glare at me all he wants, I'll come and go when I want to, he better keep his lip zipped, because he needs my money and I'm not going to put up with any more of his shit, that's for sure, You can count on it, stupid.

"I'll suck vitamins out of dog shit before I beg anything out of you."

He said that.

I want to say, so eat it. Eat snot, too, while you're at it. Eat bloody Kotex. I bet he sent her to talk to me, because he's right, he can't ask for anything from me. So why do I feel bad? They didn't give me so much. I feel crawly, hives climbing my neck. I want to cry. I tried to buy a beer last night for a guy that bought me two already. He's a friend, from work, but I couldn't do it. When the bartender said how much, I opened my purse looking, but said, "Sorry, I didn't bring any money." Because I know I have to give them what I have. What did they give me? A shitty room, shitty clothes, everything shitty. And I have to give them everything. I want to give them everything. I can't let anything happen to them.

And he says things like that.

They gave me what they had. It wasn't much, but that's not their fault. They did pretty good considering where they came from. I'd rather die than have anything happen to them. Even him. I can't stand to think if he was sick. I don't want to give them my money, but I have to, and I want to give them my money. Because she's right, no matter how awful it ever got, we stuck together.

But why does he say those things?

"Your father was born unhappy," she'd say when we were little, "He was forty years old when he was in diapers. Born with one foot in the grave. He's morbid and that's that. You have to love him anyway. He doesn't know how to be happy like other people. They're all that way in his family. His mother used to tell us about every funeral she ever went to. I'd send you kids out of the room. How this one's eyes opened when the embalming fluid went in, or that one woke up in the grave, they know, because they found claw marks on the inside of the coffin lid. He grew up like that. All his mother ever did was talk about his sister that died, her favorite child, the dead one. No wonder he turned out the way he did. You have to accept him and love him for what he is. An unhappy, morbid man. But we had our laughs. He's got a good sense of humor. And he's a good provider."

Well, he hasn't provided anything lately, and he still talks like a rat died between his teeth. I don't get it. Nobody can *be* that way. You have to work at it. Don't tell me that remark about dogs popped in his mind. He had to think about it, get it right, before it could bloom out of his mouth. He can have anything of mine he wants if he'd stop thinking that way.

FATHER:

"You go anywhere today?"

"Yeah, I talked to some places. I'm telling you I can't believe it, there's nothing out there. You see chain link fence and padlocks. You see thirty guys lined up at the side door of places got one opening."

"Did you get in anywhere? You filled out some applications, didn't you?"

"Couple places did me the courtesy. But they got no use for grey hair, they got no use for forty-three years old. Better I have leprosy than forty-three. Fill out the application:

"'Any diseases?'

"I say, 'Leprosy.'

"'That's okay, we can live with that. Your dick didn't fall off yet, did it?'

"'Not yet.'

"'You're fine, then, don't worry. How's the eyesight?'

"I say, 'Good. Great! Call me Eagle Eye! 'Cept, well, it's a little dim now and then. Actually, my eyes fell out.'

"'We can live with that, long as you got two good hands.'

"'Well, I only got one hand left, but three good fingers on it.'

"'That's okay, there's jobs we only need your back. How many smarts you got?'

"'I been tested at cretin level, but I can perform up there with the morons if you give me a chance.'

"'Moron! Superior brains for what we need. Good, good. Let me mark that down. How long on your last job?'

"'Twenty years.'

"Twenty years, they know they got a dumb schmuck, something wrong, 'All those years, you left your job to come over here, why's that?'

"First couple times it came up I said, 'I got in a disagreement with the boss that proved unresolvable after I offered a forceful opinion.'

"'Uh, huh. What's that mean?'

"'We didn't get along.'

"I'm out of there. There's lots of sweet sheep they can hire, guys that'll crawl on their hands and knees through pig shit, smile while they do it. They don't need anybody doesn't get along. When they see my frosting up top, they need a old man that doesn't get along like they need a hole in the head."

"Honey, you'll find something. Stick with it."

"What I'm gonna do, pull the covers over my head?"

"You can't let any grass grow."

"Yeah, yeah, yeah. Getting so I don't know where to apply, though. Used to be the factory at the end of every block had a guy at the door pulling you in by the sleeve. "Come work here." These little tool and die shops, places only make the screw that holds the knob that holds the fusebox under the dashboard of your four-door Pontiacs, guys had enough orders to run three shifts a day. Those years I could have been a homicidal maniac flipping the chamber of a thirty-eight while I wrote my ap, they'd say, "You're hired." The city was humming. But I get canned, what happens my timing is wrong. You see big red signs, "Don't bother," by the side gates, don't even want you to come in. Doesn't matter if they take you on, you feel better leaving your name behind. They won't even let you do that. Twenty years, you'd think a guy's got something to sell, but they got x-ray eyes or something, see my brittle bones and nothing I do can't be done by a younger man they don't have to worry about medical claims so much."

MOTHER:

Then he petered out.

Stopped trying to wake me, didn't flop on the bed like a whale trying to rouse me or slip his hand where it doesn't belong. And that was okay, because like I say, some of us have to WORK in the morning. But then Saturday rolled around and it'd been over two weeks, because we skipped our regular Saturday, though I didn't think anything about that since there was so much you know what going on the weeks before that. I thought he needed a rest. But this Saturday he started his leering, his let's rattle the roofbeams, baby, and I thought we were back on schedule, went to bed half hour early that day like we always do when we're scheduled, to make sure we don't stay up too late, and he began his part while I got ready to receive him, but when the time came, there was nothing there. From billy goat to worm, no time flat. He was still over me, with a look on his face, surprise was what I thought it should be, or embarrassment, but it was more strained, like he was trying to blow up a balloon with a big hole in it, and nothing happened.

Looking up into his face, I said, "You should have had all your liver tonight. It's got iron. It would help here."

I was a little amazed since he never had this trouble, first time, he was deflated as a rubber balloon, hanging, nothing.

"I don't need goddamn liver."

He was still straining like he could make everything come up where it's supposed to, but he wasn't much of a husband. Nothing. Men get so upset. As a woman it only meant that I didn't have to change the sheets, so I was going to roll over and go to sleep. So? He was starting to clean the house pretty good now that he was used to sitting around. It wasn't so bad. He kept straining, I thought he was going to explode, but there wasn't anything there to explode.

"Gimme a minute, a minute."

He kept coming at me, wanting to make something happen, but if it didn't happen for him, I couldn't do his part. I'm not made that way. I'm a woman. And finally he gave up. Rolled over and lay there on his back staring at the ceiling.

"Oh, don't worry about it. There'll be other Saturdays."

"Maybe. I don't know."

What'd he mean, "Maybe." Of course there'd be other Saturdays. They come around like clockwork, twice a month he gets it, you can set your watch, and that seems to set him up fine, so what's "maybe" mean? But I found out a couple weeks later when he didn't even come to bed when I did, sat there reading a book, squirming a little on his butt, knowing it was time, and he didn't even look up from the page. What's that mean? He's not going to do his part anymore? It's not that important to me, but it's where he's got a duty to be every couple of weeks, so I know everything is how it's supposed to be. How do I know everything is fine with my marriage if he's not where he's supposed to be?

And he started to bring home more magazines, dirtier ones. I found them downstairs in the fruit cellar hidden. What's he hiding them for? And these were disgusting. Women doing things with their mouths you wouldn't make a condemned prisoner do, I don't care if he shot a policeman. He was looking at those things. I wasn't going to bring it up, thinking maybe it would help him a little, get him back on track, until I looked at the price, about three times *Playboy*, and that did it.

"I don't know what you're doing with this in my house, but I want it out of here."

He started with his he'll look at what he wants to look at, thought that would cut some ice with me. Hah!

"When you start paying your own way, fine, but don't use my money and your daughter's money to load this house with filth."

And he shut up. I never saw him shut up before. That stopped him cold, threw water on his fire, and I don't see any reason why I have to put up with it. He's sitting around here day after day with his thumb up his butt, he can do something constructive with himself. But as my mother always used to say, and I couldn't agree more, enough is enough.

I'm not going to coddle him. He wouldn't let me anyhow. He

says, "Fall down, pick yourself up. Shake the dust off your britches and continue on your way." It's time for him to show us how it's done.

And moving isn't going to help.

"There's jobs in Houston and Dallas, even for a old fart like me on his last legs."

"You're not on your last legs."

"Depends on who you talk to. Talk to the people who hire, you find out I got terminal grey hair."

"Cut it out. You're not dead. And we're not moving to Texas. The last thing I'll do is sit on a cactus in the middle of nowhere."

"Honey, this is news: There's honest to God cities in Texas."

"What are we going to do with my family, my sisters and mother, are we going to move them, too?"

"That's why God invented the postage stamp, honey, so you don't have to camp on their doorstep all the days of your life."

"I'm not giving up my family because you lost your job. And I'm not giving up the city I grew up in. And I'm not losing this house. So you make up your mind to do something because I'm not moving. Because you lost your job you think I should quit mine and chase off to where you're starting over. No seniority. Nothing. Someone must have knocked you over the head. It's not going to happen. You're dreaming."

"I might pick my ass up without you then, go where there's work and you can follow or stay. I don't give a goddamn."

"There's the door."

BROTHER:

My sister was propped on the toilet seat with her chest torn off, two craters where her breasts should have been. Her mouth hung open with all the teeth broken at the gum line, and her face wore the rictus of a scream she couldn't get out. Because she was dead. On the floor by the sink, the old lady was crouched in her bathrobe, her mouth ringed with blood, she looked up at me. She was devouring the old man's belly, who lay on the floor in front of her, moving his arms and legs like an insect trapped on his back, clawing the floor and walls, unable to escape as she dipped her head into his guts. Her head bobbed as she gnawed and tore. I haven't been able to sleep a whole night since I had that dream.

I don't know how, but these last months, since he lost his job, the old lady is getting bigger, not in her body, not arms and legs bigger, but like cabbage, a smell taking over the whole house.

SISTER:

I had a wish for it, I didn't know I had it, it was inside me glowing weak, a fire, how I wanted him to touch me, how good it would feel, him tell me it was all right and the wish so deep inside it was invisible, a weak fire that must always have been there, but I couldn't see it no matter how much I squinted my eyes because of fog and far away glowing, a wish for him to touch me so when it happened it was different than I ever imagined, when it happened neither of us all the way awake, it happening so softly and quietly I almost missed it happening, thought it was nothing until it was happening and then realizing it not like electricity, but like waves of softly flowing water washing under my skin, tingling to the surface, the whole room the whole house and then it was over as softly and quietly as it began and I had to blink and think, did this really happen?

To wish so much for something to want it and want it so much that it is part of you so deep that you don't even know it's part of you like a shadow and a shadow never asks for anything or whimpers when it runs into things or waves its arms for attention, a part of you you don't even know is there unless you look to see it.

And what happened so forbidden and frightening I should hang my head, I should enter every room weeping, if anybody found out, what that touch was and said it around and people knew what that touch was I would be forbidden.

And nothing I'm ashamed of because I didn't do anything and he didn't do anything but touch and nothing gets born of touch and nothing is hurt by touch if it's gentle and reaches deep inside with a gentle hand to bring out that secret wish making it bigger, adding to it, each touch, each stroke of fingers.

How I came in the room not awake the liquor making my eyes sleep tipping me on my feet, my steps uneven, the doorframe bending away from my hand as I walked in the room from too many drinks that I know I shouldn't have had but they were there and they kept pouring in the glass and a hand kept lifting them to my lips and I didn't taste them and I didn't think about them and I didn't get any pleasure from them, nothing more than pouring them down the drain, so does that count? does that count as drinking? pouring down the drain my throat was, easing me back into pillows that floated around my head, warm blankets that floated around me made me sleepier, but drinking still and driving the streets to get where he was to drive the streets with the lights going past my eyes the red and yellow too bright lights and signs and stores and restaurants, too bright for sleepy eyes driving through the night all the while knowing without knowing this wish inside me that I didn't know was there surprised it's there and finding it suddenly later with him when all I was thinking while I drove is how to keep from sleeping in the street in the car arms so heavy they want to drop to my sides this drive through long streets that go on for miles and miles and miles and miles and miles of lights

Into the driveway, his driveway,

Into the door, his door,

Into the kitchen, his kitchen,

The light in the front room where I see the man's legs framed in the door thinking he's not supposed to be there is never there shouldn't be there for me to see him there or him to see me or us to see each other with the doorframe bending away from my hand when I try to steady myself between the kitchen and the living room sprawled out on the couch not expecting him to touch me thinking he won't touch me the man sprawled on the couch asleep like that can't touch he sleeps there on the couch, think: was he waiting for me? was he waiting? and a tremble of fear that he's waiting but the doorframe slipping from my hand how I catch myself first so no time to be scared of him waiting for me in his house sprawled out there for me to look at though I still think I will creep past, ignore him, make him think I never crept past in the night thinking that my breath is too far away from me feels like someone else's breathing and I know that's the liquor that makes my breathing someone else's and floating with pillows and blankets around me warm it can't be bad it can't be bad sometimes to make a drain out of a throat to feel the blankets and pillows softly descending on your head and shoulders.

Sprawled out with a man's arms and a man's legs as though I don't know who he is, seeing him for the first time a man's gristle on his chin and a man's tattoos on his forearm, there, a man I have never seen who doesn't even know I'm there though he waited for me or might have waited for me and I don't care if he waited for me and thought I didn't know it was the wish, maybe the wish in me pulling me closer to the couch, this new man this never seen before man, catching my foot on the rocking chair and almost falling on him but don't to lean over him and look down on him sleeping for what reason did he go to sleep here, for me? a man waiting for me? thinking that's not scary now, that's nice that he waits for me,

To thank him for waiting for me, to say that's nice you waited, nice, should be thanked for such niceness coming out of him that he waited so long he couldn't keep his eyes open so feeling the pillows and blankets himself from waiting not from liquor but into that place where everything is pillows and blankets descending around you to thank him I lean over him to kiss him on the forehead, thank you that you think so much of me, that you think of me at all and wait, I don't know another man that waits and bend low over him to thank him with a kiss on the forehead and lips bump his head less gentle than I wanted that hurt my lips and jar his head not the thank you I wanted to give him but having thanked him anyway,

But the bump jars him and he rolls to his side, opens his eyes enough to see that even though his eyes are open they are shut back behind the eyes, sleep pillows them and they close again, but hands are less asleep than eyes and his throat groans and mumbles something too asleep to know what it is for he slips hands around my thigh

He slips hands around my thigh and almost pulls me on him where I almost tumble catch with the back of my hand the back of the couch and hands hold and touch my thigh softly and gently to almost

To almost touching me *there*, almost, and his face hurts how it frowns with the touch how I know the touch is touching him deep as me

I'm there unmoving with hands moving up and down and under my short skirt to the top of my leg where it bushes out and then the hands slow fall away from me and slide down to my knee and travel slow back to his chest where they fold under his arms, the touch over how he rolls over on his side away from me and I see that man's back and the hair climbing out of his t-shirt, sleeping and I get up and stand over him and then only then

Realizing that we touched he touched that it happened quiet as a page in an open book turning by itself

Though the book doesn't know what it did, it did what it did, and though he didn't know what he did, he did what he did, though I know what he did I'll forget what he did because the pillows and blankets are falling faster around me now and I might curl up in front of the couch if I stay there any longer and I'll forget he touched me

Because he's my father

And it's forbidden

She would forbid it and I forbid it and he forbid it so we will forget it

And it's not forbidden to forget

And it's not forbidden to sleep

FATHER:

She looked at me like I bit off the pope's nose and was using it for chewing gum. Her eyes were big and glittery and she clenched her brow so hard it turned white when I said, "What in heaven's name would possess you to do such a thing?"

"I thought it would do you some good."

"I want good, I'll get laid. Meanwhile you keep your nose out of my business."

"Guy, when your business affects the whole family, then it is my business, and it wouldn't hurt you to have some faith."

"I do have faith."

"I haven't been able to get you inside a church in years and it's what you need."

"I said I have faith. I didn't say anything about church. And who the hell gave you the license to decide what I need."

"You should believe in God. He'll help."

"I do believe in God, but I'm not sure He's helping. Of course I believe in Him. How the hell else could that tree out there dig it's roots in the dirt, or stars whiz through the sky. Nobody threw them up there. They didn't appear out of nothing. Something put them there, and for lack of a better idea, I'm willing to point my finger at this thing we call God and say, 'You did it.'"

"Like an accusation. You're blaming Him!"

"Hell, I'm praising Him. Acknowledging all He does. He keeps the salt mines from collapsing under Detroit. He keeps our miraculous hearts pumping well enough so we can outrun most of what chases us. Keeps blind old retired bastards on their side of the white line, because God knows they can't do it by themselves. Something keeps the fragile strings of this world in place, and it's this idea, 'God', that does it."

"Idea! God's not an idea. God is God."

"Well, honey, I bow to your superior logic. But I gotta say this, what He looks like or how He behaves in His own house, how He wants us to behave, I don't know. I don't know if He's got a belly button or a zipper, if He's got a dick hanging off Him or a committee of dicks. I don't know the best way to praise Him, singing out loud or pretending He don't exist so He don't get self conscious. I don't know. But I believe in Him."

"What kind of belief is that? You don't do anything for Him."

"Who says you gotta do something? You think He's waiting around for us to lick His ankles? He's got almost as much to worry about as the head of GM. Here's the way I believe in Him: I take nothing from no man and have no man take nothing from me. I try to walk in my own direction and only give a shove if some stupid son of a bitch is blocking my way and can't explain why. Except for disease, which is a blemish on an otherwise perfect creation, a mistake God made . . ."

"God doesn't make mistakes."

"How do you know?"

"Because He's God."

"Oh, you got me again. But if He did, say He did, disease would be it. It's like He was squatting on the crapper when it came up, like a telephone ringing, and He didn't want to get up to take care of it. But other than that, His creation is perfect. Pigeon shit is perfect in its whiteness and splatter. Falling down gravity hurts the stupid as much as it ought to. The way freezing wind stings and numbs and finally lulls you to sleep till you're dead is brilliance beyond Beethoven. That's the way I believe in God, and I don't see He needs anything from me."

"That's nothing. Anybody can believe that."

"Yeah, probably true. Certainly true. My belief is based on what anybody can see. I don't try to carry 'God' beyond the limits of things I can put my hands on. My belief allows me to leave the other guy alone and I expect the same. I don't need a church to tell me how to think this out. I did it all on my own."

"That's why you do need the church."

"Why, so some anemic bastard never been laid can tell me how to live my life?"

"So you understand God a little."

"Nobody can't understand God if they open their eyes. The church is religion and religion is the way man has of fucking up the idea of God. Because there's nothing one man has tried to teach another man that he hasn't fucked up in the telling, and religion is no exception. I prefer my God-given ignorance."

"Is that the reason you treated him the way you did?"

"I wouldn't have treated him any which way if he didn't stick his nose in my business."

"I asked him to."

"Then when *you* stuck your nose in my business. When I saw that bloodless bastard banging on the door, dressed in black, with his collar turned backwards, I figured he got the wrong house. I pointed across the street, said, 'Over there, old Mr. Piste, you want him. Talk to her,' Mrs. Piste was backing out the drive. Okay, Piste's got the cancer crab gnawing his insides, figured that priest was here to give him his last rites, the moment had arrived. Never occurred to me he was here to give me mine."

"Don't exaggerate. You're always exaggerating. Tell me what the hell went on here."

"What's to tell? He stuck out his fingers that drooped like damp spaghetti, said, 'Your wife asked me to stop by. I'm Father Carey.' He's a new one. I hadn't seen this one before. Not that I'd know if I did. They all look the same. I'd say a vampire about half done sucking on him got bored of the taste, walked away and left this wilty thing behind."

"He's been at the parish four years now."

"That long? My, it's been a while."

"What's why I'm telling you to go to church."

"I'm not going to church if he's an example."

"Tell me what happened."

"Nothing. I said, 'Sorry, father, she's at work. Come by on a weekend, you might catch her."

"That's it?"

"Well, honey, if that was it, he wouldn't have called you bitching about me, would he? He's got to be real limp to whine back to you. He said, 'Actually, she felt it might be useful for me to chat with you.' He said that. You believe it? My side of town, we talk. Talk or shut up. Or yell, which is the special way we communicate with children. People with butlers chat. We don't chat. I said, 'Sure thing, father, I was thinking I feel like a chat.' I swung the door back and he came in.

"I said, 'If this is about the envelope, father, I can't up the envelope right now. We got money troubles. I'm sure she's putting in as much as we can afford,' thinking he'd been pestering you for more dough and you wanted me to deal with him. Bastards never wonder where their next meal is coming from, don't have kids in their hair, what do they care who they lean on?"

"Guy, tell me what happened, for crying out loud. You don't have to give me the philosophy of the world while you do it."

"He said, 'Well, no, it's not about your weekly offering. It's about a personal matter.'

"I said, 'You got a problem you're dealing with, father?"

"Well, yes, in a manner of speaking, yes,' he said.

"I said, 'Well, you brought it to the right place, I'm here to help, father, you can spill your guts to me. It won't go no further than the two of us."

That even made her smile a little bit.

"He had a crinkle around his eyes, trying to figure out what I was saying, and then he chuckled. 'No, I don't have any problems.'

"'You don't have any problems? None? Father, that is a problem. You don't know what you're missing. Problems is how I know I'm alive. I always feel alive when I got a pain in the ass. On the other hand, I can see it would make things pretty calm. Way I feel sometimes with all the problems I got to deal with, I feel like I ought to divorce my wife, ship my kids to an orphanage and take vows, if it'd get me away from all the problems. That's what happens to priests, eh? They don't get any problems.'

"'Of course we have problems.'

"Now we're getting somewhere, father. You sit down here and tell me about it.'

"He said, 'It's not my problem. It's your problem.'

"I said, 'Well, yes, it is, father, that's why you brought it to me isn't it? So I can take your problem and solve it. Isn't that what a counselor is supposed to do, make your problem my problem and solve it?'

"He said 'Let's start over. I'm a trained social worker as well as a priest.'

"'That must make it doubly frustrating not being able to solve it.'

"'Your wife asked me to talk to you about *your* problem.'

"I said, 'What problem?'

"He said, 'I was hoping you'd be willing to share that with me.'

"He's looking at me and his neck around the collar was swelling up, changing color.

"I said, 'How can I share when I don't know what we're talking about?'

"He said you told him I lost my job.

"I said, 'You got another one for me. That'd solve a big problem.'"

"Why do you have to put people through these inquisitions?"

"He's the one asking questions. He took a deep breath and plunged on. I have to give him credit."

I'm laughing, remembering the priest. She's not.

"Priest said, 'Your wife said since you lost your job, you've been acting different.'

"I said, 'Okay, okay.'

"He said, 'You admit you've been acting different? Do you want to talk about it?'

"'Yeah,' I said, 'I do. Since it's got her so upset we ought to talk about it.'

"He gets this holier than thou grimace, I want to bust his chops with a chalice. I sat there looking at him leaning forward, breathless to wedge himself in my business. But he was right, since I quit work, no question, I been acting different. I could feel the emotions reaching right down through my bones. He said, 'Don't be ashamed. I'm a priest and I've heard everything under the sun there is to hear,' which I seriously doubt, knowing some of the stuff I know from listening to guys in the Marines, stuff that'd make a bishop faint. He's licking his lips, 'How have you been behaving different?'

"I said, 'Well, I admit since I lost my job, it's got her all upset, but look, here's the problem, since I lost my job, I haven't been reporting to work.'

"He said, 'Jesus Christ!'

"Now, father,' I said, 'You tell me one of your problems.'

"I liked him better after he said, 'Jesus Christ.' I didn't know they were allowed to do that. I thought it might be nice to chat a while longer, seeing as how we were making progress in our relationship, but he had to rush off and sprinkle holy water on somebody's coffin or something."

MOTHER:

He's a child. All he does is play. He plays with me, he plays in the house all day, nothing but play, play, play. Now he plays with that priest. Well, la de da. I've had it up to here. I'll straighten him out if it's the last thing I do. He won't make fun of me like that ever again. Father Carey is a PRIEST. You don't make fun of a PRIEST. He studied God all his life so he can help us. You let him help. That's his job. He'd be better off if he listened to people who have jobs. They know what they're talking about. I didn't marry him to sit on his ass all day. That's not the agreement. I didn't agree to that. My income is extra. His job is the main income. He'd better get with the program. Mister, get with the program, you hear me? I'm not your dumping ground. You got a load on, you won't dump on me whenever you feel like it. You got a 'wad', disgusting, disgusting talk, pig talk, fly right or that 'wad' can rot where it belongs. You shoot off your mouth like that then you sure aren't going to shoot your wad. Not at me, buster. Get that straight right now. Treat a priest that way, I could brain him. He's laughing about it. He laughed through dinner. I thought he was going to slaver down his chin and after dinner, after dinner, suddenly behind me, at the sink, grabbing my waist, pinching my butt like he's got a right to pinch my butt when all he does is play.

He's got no right to grab me like that when he doesn't have a job. You make an income, mister, you get some of this. Not before. But he kept right on coming at me. What was I supposed to do? Lock myself in the bathroom? I had to give in and while we were going our business, he's laughing to himself and taking extra long to shoot, to wear me out, to annoy me when he knows I have to get up in the morning, laughing through it like he's having a high old time. Well, mister, so you know, in the future, you want the candy, you pay the piper. So you know, mister, you have no right to pleasure yourself with me like a dumping ground until you acknowledge that I am the breadwinner and I keep things together around here. Not you. You're so much furniture. You're an old piano bench needs dusting, that's all you are.

He's lucky. He's my husband so I love him, I do, all the way, it comes out of me like it's supposed to come out of a wife. But you don't love a child the same way you love a husband, and he's a child. What right does he have? What separates a man from a child is a man goes to work. He said it a million times. I want to tell you something, mister, that's one thing you said that I believe. He could at least say thank you. Acknowledge the sacrifices. Some husband. He doesn't even have a job. He better tuck that thing in his pants until he starts showing a profit. I didn't like his spell of not having it up where it's supposed to be, but it was more suitable for someone who's leading the same life as a bum, only he has a comfortable chair to do it in.

Make fun of me.

It wasn't easy to talk to Father Carey. It was embarrassing to say my husband lays around like a throw cover on the couch, leading the life of Reilly, asking him to come over here. I made Father promise he'd keep everything quiet as a confessional. But how do I know he'll keep it to himself when he gets treated like that? That priest was so mad I bet he blabbed all over the rectory.

And *he* gets a kick out of it.

He gets big as the Fourth of July. Proud as a peacock he threw a priest out of the house. Used to be he'd cash a check he'd feel that way.

I have a right to control here. Do you hear me, mister? I'll go in there and tell him. I have a right.

All his opinions, know it all.

I hope his thing falls off, because it rises up and gets in the way of what should be a very calm marriage. After all, at our age, that thing shouldn't get in the way. I thought I made it clear I was throwing cold water on it until he got himself straightened out. And that means WORK, mister.

SISTER:

I didn't want to get out of bed. When she was banging on the door. I never want to get out of bed. I could spend the day there. Not thinking. Warm. Nothing. But the difference, or stirring, or maybe only knowing the difference, so I got up. No complaints. Careful, no complaints. Everything in order. The way to deal with this. The best way. Doing everything right keeps them back. I should have thought of this years ago. When I do what they say, when I do it when they say it, they leave me alone. I should have done this years ago. Not so bad finding clothes and getting ready right away. Fight through the webs. The veils. The way my tongue rolls around like it has nowhere to go. It has places to go. Before she gets violent with the door. Before she gets worked up. Get moving. Easier.

"My, oh, my, miracles will never cease. Look what crawled out of its hole."

This is the way. Dressed and in the bathroom and who's going to notice me when I do everything right. Nobody. She's washing the bathroom floor already. Can't get in. Lean on the doorframe, waiting.

"Are you all right? Are you sick?"

"I'm okay."

"Why'd you get up so early?"

"I thought I'm supposed to get up."

"You are. You're not sick?"

"No."

"Then get out of the way." She's pulling the bucket, crawling on her knees so her feet are kicking me. I back into the hallway. "I didn't expect you up so early."

Throwing off her schedule, she'll notice. Be careful.

Coffee and cigarettes while I get ready.

There's a normal life to lead. If I dress right and shower when

I'm supposed to and eat what I'm told, they'll forget I'm here. Everything will be okay, the same, nothing will change, I'm the same person in my dress. Look, I'm picking up my purse! And by the curb out there, my car. Same car I drove yesterday and the day before. Who's going to notice me when everything is exactly like it's supposed to be. I get up and go about my business and don't make any noise and don't offer opinions and don't leave behind a mess.

"Christ! Honey, she's emptying her wastebasket. Hallelujah! She's seen the light. Praise the Lord and pass the Jim Bean!"

Clean up a little, not much. They'll notice. He lifts his coffee cup to me when I empty the basket. The closest he's come to saying he likes me I can remember. Because I'm emptying the basket. See how easy it gets, how ordinary we can be, if I do everything I'm supposed to do. There are formulas. Rituals to all this. Why didn't I see it before?" How could it have taken me so long to see that all I have to do is show up on time, and not say anything I'm not supposed to say and I'll fit in nicely, like a knickknack sitting on a shelf. Who notices after a while? And there is no difference at all. Everything will go on like normal. It's a very orderly life if I live it by the rules, and we all agree on the rules of this life, how to stand, how to look, what to say, where to go, how long to stay, how to eat, how to wipe my face with a napkin and ask to be excused, how to be fixed and tidy and trim. There is, as she says, "method to the madness," and I know the method, I know how to help coordinate the system, do my part with an orderliness and precision that will make be blend in like a blade of grass. And ignore the stirring, the difference, and if I don't notice and do what I'm supposed to do, they'll ignore the difference and do what they're supposed to do, and it will all follow the regular pattern, and nothing will have to change.

There are things to be done.

"What brought you back to your stall so soon?"

"I didn't feel like going out after work. I feel like reading or watching TV."

"That's very good, honey."

"Christ, I forgot what she looks like. Three days in a row. You keep this up I might remember your name."

I don't want you to remember my name. I want to be a mild

breeze that goes through the living room nobody looks up to see, nobody notices, a part of the family nobody even glances at, and that way there's no difference, we can all go on. I don't want you to remember my dress or the way I combed my hair or when I left or when I came back.

"Children should be seen and not heard."

I won't be seen and I won't be heard. And I'll go to work and do my job quietly like they want me to, not frowning and not smiling, with no look on my face at all, a blank face, my real face plastered over with white cement and I do what I'm supposed to do, come and go when I'm supposed to, a good girl, a good girl doing what a good girl does, and when she does nobody has to notice her and everything can go on forever and ever and ever the way it always has.

I'll be good, so good you won't ever remember me being so good, so really really good you'll always love me, you'll want to hold me on your lap and read me stories and nothing will change, it won't ever have to change because your good little girl does everything she's supposed to. A simple, little girl. With funny jokes. Little tiny jokes that are only really funny to a little girl. Who likes to skip on the sidewalk and sit under the kitchen table with her dolls, but only between meals, not when anyone is at the table, no, that would be bad. And I'm good. A good girl. I won't spill milk, and I'll keep mustard off my blouse. You don't have to tell me to comb my hair or brush my teeth, that's how good I am. You won't even have to tell me to buckle my shoes. And then there'll be no difference at all. I'm the good, clean, modest little girl who keeps her hands folded in her lap and reads from her Sunday Missal all through mass and doesn't kick the kneeler, the immaculate little girl so innocent and delicate and blameless you want to keep her near you, close where you can talk to her and play with her and protect her.

I'll do everything right if you'll not notice me and let me go on and on and on like there's no difference, no stirring.

Because any stirring is a mistake that happened to somebody else, through somebody else's carelessness and I don't blame you for getting mad at her. She should be punished. No wonder you want to turn her out of the house. I'd want to throw her in the street if she was mine. I'd turn my back on her. I couldn't even look her in the face I'd be so ashamed.

"Can I help?"

"Sure, start with the pots and pans."

If I do everything right then it's not happening. It's happening to someone else. I want it to happen to someone else. If I keep quiet and demure. If I listen when I'm spoken to and only open my mouth when I'm asked a question. If I breathe through my nose. If I keep my hands at my side. If I stand up straight. If they see what good posture I have. Then this is not happening. It never happened. Can't happen. I'm a good girl. See me line up my shoes in the closet. See me turn off the lights when I leave the room. The drawers aren't gaping open, uh, uh, see how I close every one of them after I take out what I need.

But no matter how hard I try, no matter, there is a difference.

And it's not happening to someone else, it's happening to me.

And though I keep everything in order and make my bed when I get up and they're pleased and happy and she even smiled at me when I rinsed out her dishes for her, and they don't know anything, they're ignorant as ignorant doorknobs, as little children, as little ignorant mongoloid children.

Oh, no, don't ever say that, "mongoloid." I didn't say "mongoloid." In the name of the Father and of the Son and of the Holy Ghost, I didn't say that, and though they don't know anything and are happy with me, they see I'm turning over a new leaf, they'll know soon enough, no matter how I try.

And I don't know what to do.

And I don't know who it was. The one with the brown hair or the blond hair or the black hair or the curly one, or the one that said he was Italian, the stallion, or the Greek who played basketball or the drunk one or the skinny one or the skinny drunk, or if it was love or hate or indifference or a way to dump a load or if he thought of me or someone else or a girl in a magazine or if it was a jab, then zipped and gone, with me staring at the bathroom door while he washed off, or a long, lingering slow motion when minutes stretch longer than spools of thread, maybe rocking slow was what made it happen.

And I don't know if it happened when I took it inside me or in my hand or in my mouth and swallowed, no telling because things like this don't happen to me, they can only happen through impossibility, through some touch deeper than all the others, a touch that always existed even before it happened and after it happened it keeps on existing. And maybe it's something God said had to happen and I'll explain it to them that way and they'll understand. It had to happen.

And I believe it was Jeff who came around five or six times and who listened to me talk, who was nice and slow and nothing like what's supposed to happen took place, I don't think it did, I don't remember it taking place, but I got drunk, too, so who knows? Jeff who held me and when my blouse opened, his shirt opened so magically it was like a whisper being picked off me, barely a sensation, a feeling sweet and kind like being brushed all over with angel feathers, and he muttered low in a singsong and I don't remember anything happening with him but him holding me and when my shirt came off his pants flew away carried off by finders I never saw and the singsong kept up and the rocking began like waves against a rowboat, and if it happened with him in the way they say it happens to make something like this happen to a girl, then it only happened one time, because he was the sweet one, the gentlest, and I bet it didn't even happen from that one time, but from holding hands, because when he lay against me and he talked his singsong, his melody words running through me, sometimes he only held my hand and that's all, though our clothes had flown away and we were laying there with each other and nothing but skin and hands held and singsong desire between us, I bet it happened through our hands, or it was carried like dandelion seed on his singsong into my ear and journeyed through me and nothing else could have made it happen because only he held me close enough and listened to me and held me with love, because it takes love for this to happen, even short time, never to be repeated love, only he got so far inside me, none of the others, because when it came to touching this deep inside me, I blocked their seed, I did it quietly, secretly, so no one knew, with my mind.

FATHER:

That was a tough time. I couldn't get Henry to stand up. I coaxed and cajoled him, said, "C'mon, old friend, you never deserted me before. You always been there with your boots polished, with a ripe, ruddy grin on your face, at attention when I needed you." I couldn't understand it. He was lethargic, an old, half dead dog of a dick. He was on extended vacation. Problem was he was unextended. The only thing he wanted to do was pee. I thought he might have leukemia or broke his knee or something. He's been a good soldier, always, even times I've been too drunk to stand up myself, and there's been some serious drunks, wobbles to his feet, swaying toward heaven, when I need him.

"Henry, old pal, old buddy, what's wrong. You ain't talking to me any more? You on a sitdown strike? You want a raise, better conditions, looser pants, let it be known, my friend, you shall have it. I will deny you nothing."

I found myself looking askance at him when I was in the shower. I'd hold him in my hand, shriveled and soaked and soaped to fare thee well, and I'd run through the best times me and him ever had together. I'd treat him to some thoughts I keep strictly to myself for emergency situations, bristling with spice and raunch, but he hung there like an old, wet, oily rag.

"Henry, Henry, Henry. Hey, Henry!"

I talked till I was blue in the face; he wasn't listening.

A man spends his whole life building up a relationship, and then for no reason at all, gets snubbed.

There's nothing more disturbing to a man's peace of mind than a rebellious prick. It shattered my serenity. You can't get peace unless you get a piece, that's the way a man is built, and I didn't have the right tool for the job.

"Henry, you rotten son of a bitch. If I could trade you in, I'd do it. I'd send you to the glue factory, you tired old workhorse.

Henry, this is your master speaking!"

But no prick ever had a master. Old Henry cast his single worn out eye on me, as I stretched him inches longer, without spine; he'd wink, grin a little, and make up his own mind about the situation. A boneless boner. I couldn't figure him out. What precipitated this sudden desertion? Friendship like ours goes beyond silly insults or momentary spats. He's hung in there, old Henry has, through thick and thin, wet and dry, ugly, smelly and bloody, plunged through yeast infections that looked like they spilled out of a cottage cheese container. We're talking man's best friend, faithful in the face of the most daunting conditions, and yet he turned his back on me suddenly, completely, and for the first time in my grown up life, I found myself rubbing him like a magic lamp to get the genie to jump out. Nothing worked.

And then she made a remark that made sense out of it all.

"You have to pay the piper."

All these years I thought I was getting it for free. I don't know where I got that notion. Since I first squinted up at my old man and saw him puttering around the house I knew in my bones that nothing is free, nothing, least of all a piece of ass. I even told the boy, "You can pay at the whorehouse door, or you can pay cabs, bar tabs, restaurants, department stores and jewelers, but you're gonna pay for it, boy, remember that. And keep in mind if you pay at the door, you pay less." But this is a case of something you know in your brain that somehow don't translate down to your gut. Until you get a swift kick in the seat of your pants.

You lose your job, you know your loved ones will absorb the shock by taking a shot at your balls. That's the kind of world we live in. But she has a persistent nature and after her remark I knew she wouldn't be satisfied until my balls were snipped, pickled, displayed, discussed and dismissed once and for all. She's thorough, if nothing else. Her arms fell to her sides. I don't know how she did it, but she took the heat right out of her skin. After I touched her, I had to blow on my fingers to warm them up. There was more response coming back from the footstool when I shoved it aside to stand up than there was coming out of her. I don't need a lot of response, a little bit goes a long way with me, I can fuel my own fire, if you know what I mean, but it's like she zipped herself in a body bag and went to sleep on a morgue slab when she crawled into bed with me.

And I felt bad. I didn't have nothing to bring to the transaction, and I wanted that transaction bad, after twenty years of knowing where the grocery money was coming from and having it snatched away like that, I wanted some reassurance, not much, a few well placed up and down strokes of reassurance would have been enough. I wasn't measuring up, so before you know it, old Henry wasn't measuring up either, and therein lies the problem.

It began to dawn on me, in my guts this time, there's nothing spiritual in the transaction between a man and a woman. You bring home the bacon, she'll take care of the pork.

I got mad. Furious. When that priest showed up at that door, it occurred to me how far I'd fallen, so I shoved a finger up his ass and spun him around on the end of my fist.

And I understood that I'd been paying, and I was going to pay and there was nothing freely given and freely taken even in marriage, and I looked at her with new eyes, the eyes of someone who just stepped into the brothel parlor. I started to laugh. And old Henry smiled, too.

I figured I been making payments twenty years and it was perfectly all right for me to live off the interest. So I grabbed her ass.

CHAPTER FIVE

DAGOS DON'T HAVE TUMORS

MOTHER:

"It's frumpy. You look like a sack of onions."

"You want me to dress like this."

"No I don't. You can stop wearing pants up the crack of your ass. You can stop wearing tops so tight you can see every little thing. Your belly button doesn't have to hang out like a coin return inviting someone to stick his finger in there. And you still don't have to look like this."

"Can't you ever accept me the way I am?"

"Honey, you look like a rumpled bum."

Honestly, you hint around to not dress like a streetwalker and next thing, she's a big jumbled, rumpled mess. She doesn't have to wear big mohair fuzzy sweaters that make her into a blob. It's not neat. It's slovenly. And if she wants to look slovenly she's not going to do it around here. Why does everyone have to go extremes? Why can't they take good advice and shut up?

"You look fat."

"I do not. I'm comfortable. Why can't I be comfortable? Everybody wears these sweaters."

"You look like a beatnik. Is this your new phase, hunching around like a beatnik and bringing bums in sweat shirts around that don't even have jobs?"

"What bums? I haven't brought anyone around in weeks."

"You'll find somebody."

"Mother, how do you come up with this stuff?"

"Are you getting fat? Are you trying to cover up that you're getting fat?"

"I weigh the same."

"Well, it looks like you're putting on weight, young lady. You finally stop gallivanting around all hours of the night and next thing you're getting fat. Nobody wants a fat girl, you know."

"What makes you think I'm getting fat? I'm not getting fat."

"You don't think I can see your fanny spreading under that sweater from sitting too much. I'll tell you what to do about it. You can get down on your hands and knees and wash some floors. Start doing laundry. Try a little elbow exercise at the table, put your two elbows on the edge of the table and push back. You eat like a pig."

"I hardly eat at all."

"Oh, maybe around here. But you're packing something away when you go to work. What kind of lunches are you having? You can't eat hamburgers dripping with grease every day without that meat hanging off your bones, hanging down like a butcher shop you keep stuffing your face like that."

"I don't even have lunch some days."

"You think you can tell me you're not eating and that makes the calories go away? You're not fooling me."

I won't have a fat daughter. I watched half my family get fat and careless. So fat their thighs flapped together by the time they were thirty. Two, three kids and they're all done. Blobs. My daughter is not going to turn into a blob you have to help in and out of cars. I can see her spreading out and fattening up and she'll end up like my best friend in high school, Mardi, who turned into a blimp and can't get married if she advertised in the newspaper. That's what happens to fat girls.

"Ma, I'm skinny. Look at these arms. Toothpicks."

"That's not where it counts, honey. You're getting that middle age spread and you're only twenty years old."

I will not have it. She's going to get it through her thick head. If it's not one thing with her it's another.

"Well, fatty, tubby, you want to get a husband, don't you? What are you going to do about it?"

Her face was clouding up, a look of tragedy. I'm finally getting through to her.

"You want to be a blimp blob, or attract some nice guy you can have children with and a nice life? Because I'll tell you right now, Miss Folds of Fat, the only kind of guys you'll get when you're obese is the dregs of the barrel, guys you wouldn't want to wipe your boots on. Who wants to marry a hippopotamus?"

I wanted her to rethink her fat position.

"There's no such thing as 'pleasingly plump' to the good ones.

They want a hippo, they'll go to the zoo, Miss Tilly Two Ton. They aren't about to marry a fleshy, overfed, lumbering bag of hamburger grease."

With tears running down her cheeks, she looked at me and said, "Mother . . . stop, mother, I'm . . ."

"Fat!" I said, no sense letting up when I was finally making an impression on her, "Admit it and do something about it. Take your fate in your hands. Put down your fork and walk away from the supper table before you eat your way into oblivion. You're going to be big as a house if you keep up the charge of the fat brigade. Somebody is going to think you're pregnant and if you think you've got troubles now, wait, wait until a rumor like that catches on. You can ruin your reputation all because you can't keep your hand out of the cookies."

I've seen it happen. People start talking and the next thing the evidence stacks up against a girl. And she hasn't done anything. The way she's hiding out in her room like a frightened cockroach, it's easy to start tongues wagging. She stopped going out to these dirty bars and now she doesn't know what to do with herself. Well, that's got to end.

"Maybe you should get off your fanny and do something. Because you're not going to bars doesn't mean your life has to end. There's a single's club at the church."

"Mother, I'm . . ."

"Too damn good for them? Well, I'll tell you, you better do something or you're going to have a butt the size of a laundry basket. And the day you think you're too good to go to a dance with other decent children, young lady, you really are getting too big for your britches."

I thought a good talking to would make a difference, and it looked for a minute like it was going to, the way she was crying. If there's one thing in this family we're good about, that's talking about what ails us. Guy and I agreed when we got married, when something comes up we're not going to shuffle it in a closet like it doesn't exist like parents of our parents' generation did, we're going to say what's on our mind and like Guy says, "Let the chips fall where they may." But she jumped up, sobbing—I swear if that girl was in the Upper Peninsula, somebody'd think she was a waterfall and take her picture—ran into her room and locked the door. And I couldn't get her to come out.

I don't know why we never took the lock off that door. It occurred to us, but we never got around to it.

And there she stays.

She comes out to eat and then goes back in there. Sometimes I hear the radio playing soft and sometimes she's talking to herself. Sounds like she's playing with dolls or something. And I don't think my talk made a bit of difference because she keeps wearing frumpy, dumpy clothes that don't flatter her figure at all.

Guy says, "Let her stay in there. Who gives a shit? We should have put a padlock on the outside years ago to keep her in. Would have saved a lot of trouble. She wants to stew, let her."

But I have this belief we should all be together. Wouldn't it be nice if we could all sit down in the living room and she and I could knit sweaters and he could read and Mark could do something, lie on the floor or something?

"I don't think we ought to let her retreat from everything like this."

"She's been retreating since the day she was hatched."

"Well, I care about the way our daughter looks. She finally gets sensible, comes home at a reasonable hour, cleans up after herself. These last few months she's gotten her head on right. Now she's locked in there and dresses like a tent. I don't know what to do."

"Don't do anything. She's quiet. Forget her."

Sister:

I'll have you right here in this room, little Margaret, and no one will even know, it'll be just the two of us with no one ever interfering and telling us what to do or where to go or what to wear and you'll see, Tricia, that it'll be good, we'll play games and I'll teach you how to dress dolls and play tea party, I'll say, "Now, Alice, pour the tea," and you'll pour the tea and you'll say, "Now what, Mommy" and I'll say, "Now, Sandy, we have to make toast and then clean it all up," and you'll do it with me, and we'll have fun. I can't wait until you're here, Jamie, and I can hold you and talk to you with your eyes staring up at me, it'll be nice, will you love me as much, Anne, or will you find me boring like they do? or will you sleep all the time and I'll hold you and listen to your little breathing? Is that what it'll be like, Georgianna? cuddling and singing to one another, and you'll want to listen to the same radio stations that I do so we'll get along fine, forever, the two of us, and play in the closet. I'll sit on the shoes and you'll knock and I'll say, "Who's there?" you'll say, "It's me, Michele," and I'll say come in and we'll put on clothes and take off clothes, and you can hear me now, can't you Alise? can't you? you know how much I need you to hear me and trust me, nobody has ever done that, but you will, won't you, Beth? won't you, Mary Ann? won't you, Dorla? won't you, Carol? won't you, Teresa? won't you, Patricia? there are a thousand and one things we can do in this room and no one needs to know that you even arrived so we can stay with each other, because after you get bigger, after all the years I'll take care of you, then you'll take care of me, Kim, and there's nothing I won't do for you, Janie, I'm so glad you're coming to be with me, you're coming to a party, Sherry, Leslie, Naomi, Norma, Dorothy, Debbie, Diana, Deanna, did you know you couldn't be more wanted, welcome, a surprise party, you don't even know what to expect because you're curled up in me thinking about whether you even want to come out or not, but I'll make it wonderful for you to come out, no one will yell at you or hurt you and they won't ever call you stupid because I won't let them and you won't even have to prove you're smart to me, because I'll know, right now I know, I know you're smart and beautiful and graceful, whatever your name is, whoever you are, we'll be friends, except when you need me to be your mother, then I'll be your mother and only say nice things to you, all the time, I'll call you Miss Prindingle, Penelope, Little Girl Who Flies, wheeee, Through the Air, Miss Brown Eyes, Miss Blue Eyes, Miss Miracle, sunshine comes right out of your skin, doesn't it, doesn't it? you little wonderful trickster, you, how'd you do that?

(Oh, God help me, what am I going to do?)

there are rainbows and things to teach you about, and I'll let you hold on to my fingers when you're trying to walk, but quiet, not in your shoes, or they'll hear us, and we don't want them to hear us, do we, Miss Kettledrum? We want to be a secret they don't know about or anybody and I'll take you to work with me, like now, under my sweater and you won't make a peep, will you? and you'll help Mommy with her work, giggling very quietly against me and I'll look down my sweater at you, giggling there against my stomach and I'll smile, "What are you smiling about?" the boss will say, and I'll throw a frown up at him, "Nothing, sir," and he won't know and they won't know and nobody will know, but I have to ask you a question, don't get mad, but why did you choose me? did you look down from heaven and see me and think, "She's the one I have to go be with right now, she needs me," is that what you thought when you looked down and saw me? that was sweet, how small you are and how little you can do, but you looked down and thought, "I can help her, and so I'm going to go down to her now," is that how it happened, did you fall in love with me from a cloud up there and decide that of all the women in the whole world that are trying to have a little girl as wonderful as you, I'm the one that was going to get you.

(They'll kill me. They'll throw me out.)

because, sweetie, bubblegum, little sailor, angel, harmonica, lollipop, balloon face, Miss Blow On your Belly Till You Bust Out Laughing, rolly polly, funny bunny, you didn't pick a really good time for me, it's not an easy time, I don't know what to do with you, we can stay in this room for as long as we can stay in this room, but already you're too big to keep with no one knowing and I know you'll cry or drop a comb or giggle too loud, something will happen, they'll find out about us, I know it for sure and though we want to hide and play by ourselves forever and ever together, they'll find out sooner or later and they'll get mad, I've been here a lot longer than you, sweetheart, I know it, and I don't want that to happen to you, I don't want to see or hear any of that, so I don't know what to do, if you waited a little while, my little brussel sprout, maybe I could have figured something out, if I'd known you were coming, but I didn't, you caught me completely by surprise, suddenly there you were, whispering to me in my stomach and like a thousand birds jumping out of the grass, you were there in front of me and I don't know what to do

(How can I feed her? They'll beat me. She'll starve. How can I work? We'll starve. How can I do my job? How can I go in every day?)

and though I'm honored you chose me, privileged you chose me, I couldn't be prouder that I'm the one that you decided to come to be with, I'm frightened for us and I sort of wish you had chosen someone else, your second best choice, I'm sure there must have been another very nice girl you could have chosen, instead of me, because I think it's too much for me, you're too much for me, I'm little, too, you know, small and I need more taking care of than you can imagine, and I wish I was going to be your little girl because I know you'd take care of me and I'd know what to do to help you, how to sit on your lap and talk to you when you were frightened and how to tell funny stories that would make you smile so everything felt better for you, because I know how to be a little girl better than I know how to be a mommy, but I bet you'd be a wonderful mommy if you had me there to whisper things to you about what to do next and next and next

(Why do they hate me? What do they get out of hating me? Why did they do this to me?)

ah, don't kick, little one, don't kick, don't be mad, I'm sorry you made a bad choice, I'm sorry I'm such a bad mommy and you haven't even been born yet, but remember, I didn't choose you, you did the choosing, you better not kick me anymore, because if you had asked me, if you had any sense in your head at all you could have seen that it's hard for me to live here by myself in this house and the two of us are going to make it impossible, so I don't know where we'll go, maybe we should run away right now, tonight, when everyone is asleep, while you're still inside me and easy to carry, because you're going to be a lot harder to carry when you're on my arm and now you're getting all riled up, you're crying aren't you? are you crying because you're mad at me, do you hate me, too? are you another one that can't get enough of hating me? is that it, little one, is that why you're kicking my stomach around and treating me like shit before you even know my name? or is it frustration, are you crying for yourself? that you see what I've got and I can't give you any better, you know it, you know it, and it makes you want to stomp your feet all around my insides and tear the walls down, you want to escape? I don't blame you, I want to escape, too, oh, that hurts, my honey, hurts when you do that to me.

(It hurts when they do that to me.)

and I'll try and I'll try and I'll try, but you see, see why we have to be secret, why no one can know about you? because then they'll know how to really get to me, by getting to you, but if we're secret and nobody knows then they can't attack us, and you can be my secret weapon, what they don't know about, and while I go out you can sneak into their room and pull her hair and spit on him, or pour ketchup in his shoes and they'll never know where it came from, and if I have one little secret, something they don't know and can't touch because they don't know about it, then I'll always be safe, I'll always have one little jewel that I can keep all to myself, the one little jewel, the only thing I've had to myself, see? see, angel? you can be that one little thing that makes me strong because they don't know about it, and when I'm strong I'll be a better mommy, isn't that right? so will you keep quiet? will you pretend you're asleep all the time? will you stop growing so big, will you stay small so I can keep you hidden in the folds of my skin, deep inside where no one knows you're there but me, because I can protect you better if you're completely invisible, if you stay quietly playing inside me, and you can touch all over inside me, think of everything inside me as your playthings, but be quiet, small, hidden, secret, smothered down inside, it's the best way, the best thing, I'm your mommy, you should listen to me now, do as I say, you have to, I'm your mommy

(What will they do to me?)

MOTHER:

All I did was tell him she was getting fat and he flew off the handle. After so many years, I still cannot predict what he is going to do. He was swearing and pounding his fist on the arm of the chair so the whole house thundered.

"Fat! Goddamn it, fat! She's getting fat? Now I got it. Now I see. Goddamn it."

"I told her she's got to go on a diet."

He stopped and looked at me, and said, "A diet? You told her she's got to go on a diet?"

He started his the World Is Shit laugh that he uses when something isn't really funny, but mean.

"Of course, you did," he said.

I think if you're going to be amused you should let other people in on it. That's common courtesy. Of course, he says there's no such thing as common courtesy in this, quote, "rat's ass city," such language. Be that as it may, there's no reason he can't be courteous to his wife. He's only got one.

"Well," I said, "She'll have to eat less."

"We'll cut her portions in half."

"There's no harm when a person is getting fat."

"And if that doesn't work?"

"She can go on a fast. A lot of people have had to take drastic action to lose weight. She might be one of them."

"Forty days in the desert."

"Right," I said, "A hundred and forty days without dessert if she has to. And no salad dressing either."

"That's the spirit. We'll goddamn well starve her."

"Now, honey, don't exaggerate."

"We'll chain her to the bedpost."

"I don't think we'll have to go that far."

"We should have done it a long time ago. Baby, don't you

realize we could reach down her yap and take out every scrap of food she ate since last November, we could empty the icebox so it made Ethiopia look like a Big Boy Restaurant, and she'd still fatten up?"

He wasn't laughing anymore. He was looking at me, but he was talking to himself. "Now I know why she been moving around the house on cat feet, why she been hiding behind the furniture. She ain't slouching through the front room inviting a swat on the ass anymore, no, she been scooting through here like her pants on fire. I got the picture. Now I know why she been turning her nose up at her meat; two, three bites and she says she can't get another mouthful down her gullet. I got eyes in my head. If my honker wasn't so big, maybe somebody would have noticed them and give me credit for being able to see."

And she had to choose that moment to come home. He stopped her in her tracks with that look, and pointed at the couch.

"Sit down, goddamn it. We gonna have a conversation."

Her legs dropped out from under her like he hit her over the head with a club.

I said, "Be careful of the furniture."

She knows that kind of flopping down can break the springs. I wish she'd pay attention.

He said, "I want to know what's going on. Tell it."

"Nothing."

"Nothing, huh? What you mean, nothing? You mean nothing like nothing is going on . . . or nothing like you're afraid to talk about it. You mean we can all heave a hearty sigh of relief because there's nothing, and so we don't have to bat an eye when this nothing we got growing in our midst knocks on the front door with his goddamn suitcase in hand and wants to move in. Maybe we'll call him Nothing. That's a good name. That'll work. 'Say, who's that at the end of the table with his face in a plate?' 'Why, that's Nothing.' 'Hmmmm, looks like someone to me.' 'No, that's where you're mistaken. Big error. I'm someone and she's someone and you're someone, but that's Nothing. Nothing at all. That's his full name. Nothing at all.' What the fuck you trying to pull around here?"

She squirmed in her chair and looked from him to me and back to him and back to me.

"You think someone going to come to your rescue? Think she can save you? Or me? What kind of rescue you expect? It don't matter if I shut up or she shut up or anybody shut up. We still got this little matter of nothing to deal with. So say it."

"Say what?"

"You're knocked up, for Christ's sake. You took one too many plugs. You're in the goddamn, as they say, family way. Way, hell. You're at the end of the path. You practically got a house in the fucking suburbs. Say it!"

I couldn't believe the stupid things he was saying because she'd put on a roll around the middle.

He hit the arm of the chair so hard the ashtrays jumped.

SISTER:

I never saw her fight him so hard before. She scooped up the papers by her feet and threw them across the room. They spread out against the side of his chair. His neck got longer and his jaw came forward, opened a little so his lower teeth were showing in front of his lips.

"What are you trying to say. You can't accuse my daughter. You can't say that. She's putting on weight. She's fat. Fat, so what? A lot of people get obese like her. You start saying. Stupidest thing I ever heard. You can't get away with it. You can't do that to us. To this family. Even if I'm the only one who cares. I say you can't get away with it. What you're trying to say."

"I ain't trying. I said it."

"Well, shut up. The stupid things. Say stupid things like that."

"You got a bag over your head? You an ostrich? Head in the dirt? Open your goddamn eyes."

Like I wasn't in the room. They started at each other, and I never saw her hate him so much and he looked like he was going to grab the fingers she pointed at him and break them off. I didn't know what to do. They never fight. I never saw anything like it.

"Why do you think she don't eat?"

"She eats like a pig. She's eating us out of house and home. She's a glutton. We can't keep up," and she turned toward me and said, "Isn't that right, honey, you're a pig, right?" Her eyes wavered to him, to me and back to him, "She eats like it's going out of style."

"She ain't had a full meal in two months."

She changed her tune just like that, without missing a beat.

"That's because she's sick, she's getting sick in front of us. She's sick. Something is growing. A stomach tumor. An ovarian tumor. It can kill her. She needs a scraping. She's sick as anything, you're wrong, it happened to me, she's sick. Do something for her." She turned to me hoping I'd vomit blood or pass out to prove a point. If I could have hemorrhaged, I would have. For her. To help her out.

"And you sit around here on your ass all day thinking these things up. You had a job you'd have something better to do with yourself. You're nothing but a lazy, dirty, crazy filthy. Can't say anything nice to anybody. You can't see she's sick."

She turned to me and said, "What is it, honey, how sick are you? You're sick, aren't you?"

I shook my head back and forth and wished I had cancer. It would have been the decent thing to do.

"She's pregnant."

"You're sick, aren't you, honey?"

"She's a Dago, for Christ's sake."

"What's that supposed to mean?"

"What your mother used to say, 'Dagos don't have tumors. They have babies.'"

Mom sat next to me and I put my arm around her shoulders that were rounded down and tired, too heavy to keep up. She looked at her hands, her eyes turned inside. I rubbed her arm up and down, but she rounded over even further and then lifted her fingers up where she could look at them and started to work the nail polish off her thumbs.

Something must be haywire with my head. I wasn't normal. I didn't feel ashamed or frightened. I didn't want to run out of there. All these months, years I didn't want them to look at me. Now they were looking, they couldn't help it, they had to, and I felt quiet, like they'd turned out the light in my room, but hadn't yet shut the bedroom door. They were watching over me.

FATHER:

No use getting excited. No big deal. This is easier than it appears. These are modern times. They got knives now a doctor can trim away a little thing like that better than a prize-winning butcher. They can lop off the little fingers where that thing is hanging on to her insides and she won't feel a nick. Next day she'll be out playing basketball, go for a jog. Couple days off work and she'll be good as new, better, because she'll be minus that little bit of misguided fat. Nothing wrong with getting rid of the fat. Keeps a girl looking good. Keeps her figure nice. Don't think twice about it.

Back in the old days, before television, when everybody had nothing better to do on a Saturday night but fuck, they made big families. Didn't have any choice. Couldn't figure out how to get the knife in there right. The people who do these sort of things would put it in the wrong angle or something, chop the woman to bits. These days I understand it's easier than popping a zit. They don't even use a knife a lot of the time, from what I read, seems they go in there with a vacuum cleaner and suck it away like a piece of wet lint. Girl shakes the doctor's hand, and by the time the weekend comes, she feels so good, she's back on her back again. Like something out of a dream. The way life was meant to be. Nothing to it. It all works out for the best. These are the best of times for women. They don't have to worry about having one on each hip and one in the hatch. Don't have to have one unless they want to.

I look around now at the little kids I see playing in yards up and down the street, and think, you lucky little sons of bitches, somebody must have wanted you. No other reason for you to show up. They could have thrown you out with a juicy rubber, but no, they went ahead, then decided after that, today, when there's plenty of time for second thought, because they got knives and vacuum cleaners, decided, while you're settling into your mother that you feel pretty good, and woman thinks, "Don't mind if I do."

She didn't have to. She could have hired someone to snip you out. Cost next to nothing. Woman could spend a morning panhandling and get enough to get some doctor to do the job. A few bucks. Because doctors today are getting to be big-hearted men, and think a small price is what's needed to keep the world from overflowing with unwanted brats. Well, maybe that's a little rosy colored. Doctors are getting big subsidies to clean out cunts, so they're pitching in like Wall Street janitors. It's worth their while. They can do it in fifteen minutes start to finish, from the time they hoist the broad on the table to the time they collect her check at the door. They can be out cruising the boulevards of Grosse Pointe in their top down Benz while the sun's still high in the sky. Hell, I bet some of them fill a bucket with what they cut out in the morning, spend the afternoon out on the lake, using it for bait. This is the modern world. It's easy to fix things like this.

But goddamn if she ever wants to do things the easy way.

She was sitting there with her arm around her mother, and it seemed odd. Should have been the other way around. Strange world. She looked calm, and since it was the first time I can remember talking to her without inspiring a puddle of tears, I was calm, too. I asked, so we know what we're dealing with, "How far gone are you?"

"I don't know."

"Well, honey, don't worry about it. I can get the names of a couple of doctors, and we'll find one of them can fix this for you. You don't need to be bothered. Easy to fix. Cost a few bucks. Nothing much. But gimme a guess. When's the last time you had a period?"

"Seven months ago. Maybe eight."

That fish in my stomach flipped over before what she said kicked in all the way.

"Kid's ready for first communion, for Christ's sake. Why in the hell didn't you say something?"

I said it so loud, they both jerked upright, but I didn't yell. I waited for her to speak. Her face stayed calm, her lips steady for once. She reached up and brushed the hair away from her eyes and held her mother in her arms like a frightened child. She said, "I thought you'd make me quit work. And we can't afford it."

Some words cut through.

Some words make up for a lifetime.

MOTHER:

They're going to think that's how I raised my daughter. Well, I didn't raise her that way. I taught her to keep her pants up. This is not the way to have babies. There's a right way and a wrong way. There's a process. First you get a husband. *Then* you have a baby. It's the sort of thing I shouldn't have to tell her. She should know it. They're going to think I didn't teach her anything. I can't help it if it didn't sink in.

Don't tell Mark. He'll blab it all over the neighborhood. We can keep it quiet. She can come and go after dark. Why not? She does anyway. Nobody has to know. I didn't do this. I had nothing to do with it. But I'm going to get blamed for it. You can bet on it. They always blame the mother. They're going to look at me. How can I face them? Something like this is so dirty it gets remembered forever. It burns in the neighbors' minds for as long as they know you. But if we keep it quiet, nobody knows, the neighbors might not guess. It took us forever to guess, and I might never have known, if Guy hadn't pointed it out. She gained eleven pounds. She's still wearing her jeans. She was trying to starve the baby right out of her belly. Keep the curtains drawn. When the time comes, I hope the time comes after dark, we can zip her to the hospital when nobody is looking. She'll have to shut up no matter how much it hurts, we don't want the neighbors to wake up because of a lot of screaming. Whoosh, out of the house. No one has to know. I didn't raise her this way. Don't anybody look at me that way. I don't know where she gets it from. From those filthy magazines he reads, that's one place. I don't know. Not from me. I was good until I got married, and I expected her to be good, too. Bad blood, he pointed it out long ago. His sisters. Not my side of the family. Don't blame me. If only she can keep her mouth shut when it starts coming.

Thank God it's too late for an abortion. Jesus, Mary and

Joseph. The dirtiest kind of sin. They kill the baby right in the womb and pull out the corpse. I don't approve of that. That's a baby. A living being. You don't throw it away like a bit of chewed up gristle. You have to nurture it, even in the womb, encourage it. So she can have a good baby.

And then we can give it away.

They have agencies for this sort of thing. They'll place it with a good Catholic family. I won't have any trouble explaining why they've got to get this thing out of here: He doesn't have a job, she's weak from having it but she can't stay home, she's got to have a job, to help pay the bills, we'll go broke otherwise, they'll be able to see that, all the burden on my shoulders. I'd have to teach her everything about raising a baby and cook and work, too. I'll wear out in a year. I'd look like somebody's grandmother, and that's another reason to get rid of it. It'll wear me out. I'm not old enough to be a grandmother. Look at this face. Is this the face of a grandmother? Not bad, eh? I look better than I did twenty years ago, or almost as good. Well, not too shabby, eh? Anyway, I don't look like a grandmother. She can't do this to me. If it's around here, everybody in the neighborhood will hear it squawking. That's what babies do, spoil a good reputation. Never be able to show our heads out of doors.

How could she do this to me? She deliberately went out and got herself pregnant. Malicious. Trying to ruin me. I can't take much more. They'll be sorry when I break down. They won't have anybody to use up. I'm not an old shoe. He sits around all day. Loses his job. Hits his boss to spite me. The boy running in and out like he's on vacation. She'll have it and play momma and I'll have to do all the real work. They're trying to kill me. Put me in an early grave. It'll be me that has to do it all. And cook, too. They don't have any sense. They're confused and crazy if they think I'm going to do everything for them.

Let them whisk it away at the hospital, and she'll never even have to wipe its ass.

I said, "Maybe there are things we can do for you, dear."

Guy was looking at me like I was a baby, but I'm not, sometimes I see things he doesn't.

"Maybe there's a better way," and I looked at her, "She knows we can't afford it. Don't you dear?"

She nodded, dull as a pan.

"She knows we can't."

"Well, she's got that correct."

"Too late to go to a doctor, that's for sure, and I don't want to anyway. That's not right. But we can still give it to a good Catholic family."

She jerked like I'd slapped her. Good. It's good to wake a person up.

"Yeah, we could do that. Last thing we can do is raise another child."

"You with no job."

"You don't make hardly any money as it is."

"It costs a lot of money to raise a child. She'd have to quit her job."

"We'd be fucked."

"We'd need to find a good home for it."

"It's best, I think, so it'll be taken care of and it won't ruin her life. Or our life. Course it doesn't matter, our life."

"Our life is pretty much settled."

"That's true."

"But we ought to think about her life."

"And the child's."

"The child's life is important."

"We can't be selfish and keep it."

"Much as we might want to."

"We want to make sure we do the right thing, don't we, dear?"

She was looking back and forth between us. She dropped her arm from around me and settled her hands on her stomach.

"Right, dear?"

She waited, kneading her stomach with her fingers, then slowly, real slow at first, she began to nod, up and down, she saw the sense of it. I knew she was smart. I always said she was smart. She was finally showing it.

Brother:

They should have had one of these places in the Inquisition. A living room. Some living. It doesn't even resemble living. There's nothing like the torture they can put someone through in a living room. A few words, a nod here, a wink there. At a Living Room Inquisition, accusations can be made quietly, maybe a finger pointed, maybe not. You walk into it, see the victim, the torturers, the damage done, it's all over, knuckles snapped, back stretched, eyes seared with hot iron, you feel the air vibrating with screams that never were. The furniture, comfortable, neatly arranged, a pleasant place to entertain, not a drop of crimson anywhere, everybody smiling and going about their business. Reading. Perry Como crooning through the stereo. Diabolical. Something taking place, everything askew, I don't know what, some outrage, something so scandalous nobody mentions it. I have to guess from the evidence of quivering lips, flickering eyes, stiff conversation, piece it together. I have no idea.

You'd think I was the neighbors. Maybe I am the neighbors. Maybe I've been the neighbors all along. Kept outside, not allowed in. I circle the house looking in the windows and doors, search for something unlatched, but there is nothing. I'm part of this family. I'm *supposed* to know what goes on here. I thought I was part of it. Who am I? What kind of family is this? What's happening? As if the family was formed before I was even born. I was just added on. Silence. Their mouths are sewn shut, but I see the stitches, why stitches unless there's something to keep quiet, away from the world? I can understand that, of course, we don't want the world to know, but me?

They talk to her using strange sounding words, "Dear" and "Sweetheart," why? She turns away when I come toward her and shuts the door of her room. Her face says, "Not now." If not now, when?

The old man and the old lady treat me like I'm crippled. The old man flips me the car keys, says, "Boy, take off. Have a good time." Why? Usually he says, "Get out of here, and listen, shithead, don't leave pecker tracks on the back seat." The old lady comes up behind me and smooths my hair, petting me like a dog, sighs, tired. I don't understand. They don't say anything. But I know. We all breathe the same infected air, I *know* something is going on.

I feel like I'm being tortured, yet I know I'm not the victim. How do I know? I know. Claustrophobia dreams: Swimming in an aquarium filled with oil, blackness, the oil on fire, I bump into scraps of my own flesh melted off the bone. What's going on?

Until he told me.

"Sit down, goddamn it. We gonna have a conversation."

My legs went out from under me. I didn't know what I'd done wrong, but that voice, it can do it to anyone in the house, make our legs fail.

"You know something's going on around here?"

"Yeah."

"You know, huh? Then let me tell you, we're gonna give it away. Now get out of here."

He'd done that same thing when he'd talked to me about the birds and bees. I was twelve years old. He said, "You know how babies come to be?" I didn't know anything, but I was too stupid to allow myself to appear stupid, so I said, "Yeah, I know all about it." He said, "That's good. That's what's gonna save you from the same trap your old man fell in, if you remember this, and you remember it, boy, or I'll kick your scrawny ass all the way downtown and back: Use a rubber. Got that?" I nodded. I didn't know how babies were made, and now I knew there was something else I didn't know, a rubber? He picked up the newspaper and continued reading.

This time I said, "Dad, what's going on?"

"I thought you said you knew what was going on."

"I know something is going on, but I don't know *what* is going on."

"Then why'd you sit there and act so goddamn smart about everything."

"I don't know."

"Between you and your sister, I don't know which one of you

don't know more. I don't know which one of you is the I-don't-know champion. Jesus Christ, which one of you is more ignorant, I don't know."

"Me."

"Shut up."

"Dad, what's going on?"

"Your sister spread once too often."

"What are you talking about?"

"She got knocked up."

"I don't get it."

"She's bloat bellied. Got a brat in her gut. She's growing a chimp. Get it?"

"She's pregnant!"

"Jesus, the light goes on. I thought I'd have to send you a certified letter, smoke signals, hire a translator. What are you, dense?"

"How'd she do that?"

"Boy, I won't have this conversation with you right now. I thought you had some idea how that thing between your thighs works. Holy Christ, you don't know by now, you got trouble. It's not complicated. It don't take a genius. In fact, stupidest asshole on the street, some guy needs written instructions to pick his nose, even he knows how to use it. It don't take a third grade education, so how come you don't know how something like this happens?"

"I'm not stupid."

"Fooled me, way you're talking. So you know, huh? You're not going to bring home a surprise relative of your own, are you? You working on it now? Mother help me, I raised a couple rabbits."

"Dad, for God's sake, when's she due?"

"Week after next, give or take a day. Provided she don't have a lazy spell and put it off another four or five months."

"My God, she's gonna have a baby."

"No, she ain't gonna have a baby. I said she's pregnant. That don't mean she's gonna have a baby."

"What's she gonna have, a hamster?"

"Don't get smart with me, you little shit, pay attention. Your mother and me talked it over with her, went through the options, this is not easy for us, we're talking about our first grandchild here, our own flesh and blood, but we went over the possibilities, and she felt, and we agreed with her, that the baby should go up for adoption. That way nobody's life is ruined by this. This was very hard for us. You don't know how hard this is. She pointed out we cannot afford to have another mouth to feed. We're in pretty tough shape, and she's got to work. And she's too young to have a baby. You can see for yourself this is the best option. It's tearing us apart, but we're going to go along with her and give up the baby."

"Like it never happened."

"Yeah, in a couple weeks, she'll have the baby and they'll take it away and it'll be no more than a bout of illness, a short stay in the hospital for her. I'm telling you this so you know. But you got to realize that it's nothing in our lives, one minute in a long life, and don't have to mean one thing or another in the course of time."

One more baby, another child is nothing in the course of time. Another pebble on the beach. Nothing. Nothing. A child is nothing. So it's all right to pass it along. It. Not he or she. It. The world will change, but we'll know nothing happened. Thou shalt not kill. No killing here. Thou shalt not ignore. That's the way the Commandment should read. Thou shalt say what you see. Admit what you've done. There will be a hole in our lives. How can I see that and no one else?

SISTER:

Teddy bear? Puddle jumper? Miss Happiness? I have good news for you. Are you awake, are your little eyes awake? Are your lips giggling? Good news, pumpkin, comes with a smile, are you smiling?

"Yes, Momma."

We've talked it over and we're going to make the perfect home for you, we've got it all figured out, how you made a little mistake coming to me from your cloud, how you could have chosen a little better, remember how we talked about it?

"I remember, Momma."

And now you're almost here and we don't know what to do, how can we feed you when we don't have jobs ourselves? Did you ever wonder about that when you were looking down at us from above? I bet it never crossed your mind, because you're sweet, you're unworried, you think it's enough to love each other, don't you? It is, but there has to be a little more, too, bunny, did you think of that?

"No, I didn't think about anything but being with you, Momma."

Well, we're going to find the perfect momma for you, a good Catholic family momma, and we're going to give you to her, isn't that nice? She'll love you every bit as much as me, and she'll be able to give you everything you ever wanted, and you'll love her and she'll love you, won't that be wonderful?

"It sounds wonderful, Momma, but . . ."

Wonderful? It's really wonderful. Can you imagine having all the dolls you ever wanted to play with and a momma who doesn't have to work so she can be there with you all the time, that's how good your life is going to be, a life so good I wish I had a life that good, doesn't that sound good?

"It sounds good, Momma, but does it mean I won't see you?"

No, no, no, it only means you won't see me as much, cuddles, not as much, it means you won't have me there in the house with you, but when you're driving in the car with your new momma, on a shopping trip to buy you lots of new dresses, won't you like that? New dresses? You might see me out the window, and you can wave to me, or when you go to the grocery store with your new momma, you might see me passing down the cereal aisle, in the other direction, and maybe I'll reach out and touch your hand, or maybe I'll be so absorbed in shopping, I won't see you. Then you can reach out and grab my scarf and I'll see you and you'll see me in little ways.

"But I don't want to see you in little patches, Momma."

Of course, you don't. But it's something you have to get used to. You know what they say, they say you can get used to anything, and before long you won't even think about me. That will make me sad. But it won't if you promise right now, right now promise that you'll think of me every night before you go to sleep, will you do that, sparrow?

"I'll think about you every day, all day, Momma. I won't ever stop thinking of you, but, Momma?"

Yes, cabbage?

"I don't want a new momma."

I know, kitten.

"No momma will ever be as good as you."

Honey, don't be that way.

"You're my momma, I want my momma."

You're getting yourself worked up over nothing, cookie, there are lots of ways to live, lots of wonderful ways, you think you have to be with me, but there might even be a better life without me, did you ever think of that?

"I don't want a better life."

You're getting all worked up and you shouldn't do that. There's no reason, pudgeball, twinkles.

"How can you call me nice names when you're going to give me away?"

I don't want to give you away, God help me, I don't. I love you, too, but I talked it over with them, they said it was the only way. It's what we have to do.

"We don't have to do it, Momma, do we? Say we don't have to."

You're breaking my heart, twiddles. I don't want to give you away. I promise you with all my heart, I don't. I want to keep you, too. I want you to always feel this close to me, I want to share the same beating hearts, share every meal like we do right now.

"Will it hurt, Momma, will they hurt me?"

No, silly, it won't hurt. Nothing will hurt. You'll be with good people who will always take care of you.

"How do you know, Momma, do you know them?"

No, I don't know them. But they say they only give little girls to nice people and you're the best little girl ever, aren't you?

"Will I have clean sheets, Momma? Will they hold my hand? Will they know when I'm afraid, like you do, Momma, like you know when I'm afraid and you talk to me?"

They won't know everything I do. They can't know everything because I grew you in my belly. Nobody will ever know you like I do, oh God, what will I put in my belly when you leave me, dead leaves? Bloody sheets? How will I ever fill my belly again when you leave me?

"Don't make me go, Momma, please, please, Momma, I'll be good, Momma, like you promised, I'll promise, forever, Momma, and ever."

You have to go. We talked it over. It's what they said. We have to. It'll hurt them if we don't give you away.

"What about me, won't this hurt me?"

It won't hurt you. I'd never do it if it hurt you.

"What if they hit me?"

They won't hit you. They wouldn't dare.

"How do you know?"

They wouldn't.

"Do you know them?"

No, I don't know them, but . . .

"Then how do you know? How can you be so sure?"

I'm sure. I think I'm sure.

"Why aren't you acting like my momma? I can't stand it. You're acting like you're not even my momma and I'm still in you. Who are you, Momma, who are you? What kind of momma are you? Are you really *my* momma?"

Stop this, they're making me. They're making me.

"Make them stop."

I can't. I can't. I'm not strong enough.

"Momma, don't give me away, please."

Brother:

She sat at the kitchen table, her stomach pushed her away from the edge, her sweater many sizes too big. I should have guessed. She was a house, residence of someone I would never know. Her arms rotated around the bulge, her small head perched above. Pouched and bubbled by the parasite in her stomach, she rolled her shoulders, dipped the left one, pushed a hand into her ribs; the parasite gobbled more territory. She was a shell, a habitat, a beanpod skin to be split and discarded. Another being would step out of her. I couldn't tolerate looking at her. I didn't want to touch her. I was afraid she had become something that I would never know, would never want to know. I wanted my sister back, not spread like the skin of a drum beaten by that wordless musician inside her. Nothing would be left of her. I'd heard the tale of my own delivery often enough to know a woman is ripped and thrashed empty on the birthing table by the wildly violent thing that sloughs out of her in a torrent of blood and membrane, child and mother both scream at the savage disjunction.

She had gone far away from me, on a journey so distant my letters would never arrive. No telephone could tag her. I tore a napkin in small pieces, balled the strips black in sweating fingers and flicked them in the ashtray on the table next to the old man's place.

She was saying, "You want to know why I didn't tell you, it's hard to believe: I didn't know it was happening myself. It's true. Before I realized it was happening to me, it'd been happening for months. I missed a period. Is this grossing you out? Sorry. I missed a period, but that happens, sometimes I miss one, or have one so light it doesn't matter. Then I missed another one. I had a check up before I left the Service, a test to see if I was pregnant. I don't know why I had it. I couldn't be then, I knew, because I'd never done anything with Jack, hugging, making out, you know, but I'd never done it with him. Big deal, I was clean. But I got the test anyway. I was being extra safe. So when I came out of the Service, I forgot the whole idea of getting pregnant. I didn't think about it. And then it happened with this one guy, only one guy, I swear, it only happened once, can you believe my luck? One time and this happens to me. One measly time. I didn't even want to. He made me. Remember the guy who moved to Texas, well, right before he moved, he made me, he forced me to, Mark, I didn't want to. I'll tell you the truth: It was awful. I was good for so long. And then he got me drunk so I hardly knew what I was doing, he started pushing me around and suddenly it was over. I mean I was scared when he started pushing me around. He hit me across the face. His roommate was in the living room with his date, I yelled, but nobody came, and I was afraid, and then suddenly it was over. I wanted to kill him. I know you want to kill him, too, but I don't know where he is. He's lucky I don't. Boy, I'd slap him with this baby. But anyway, there I was, stuck. And I remember thinking, is this the big deal sex everyone is always talking about? Don't make faces. Really. You're going to have to learn all this someday anyway. I thought, if this is all it is, then I can do without this forever. That's why I never had any trouble passing it up later, guys would want to, every guy wants to, but I'm good at keeping them at arm's length. I light up a cigarette and blow smoke in their faces. That turns them off. Or I start to laugh. They can't stand it when you laugh at them. You'll see, if your girlfriend ever laughs at you. But this one time. Drunk. Wham, bam. Sorry, that's what they say in the Service, wham, bam, and I thought, one little one with this weinie, wimpy Go-run-to-Tex-*Ass* isn't going to matter. I forgot it ever happened. And when I started missing periods, you wouldn't believe it, when I started missing periods, I thought it was my nerves kicking up, that's what Mom thought, too, I asked her about it, she said when you go through something like what I went through you can get irregular, so I didn't think anything about it. I woke up one day, my stomach was getting bigger. I thought, maybe I am, maybe I am, but you know how my mind works, I blocked it out, forgot it, something bad that I didn't want to know. I'm telling you, it almost surprised me as much as it did you when Dad pointed it out.

"Mark, you've got that look on your face. What's wrong? This is okay, really, it'll be over soon."

"I'm afraid of you."

"Afraid of what? Afraid of what's inside me? Afraid to touch me?"

I felt made of cardboard. Set me up in a grocery store, point me to the peas. I'll stand there till they sweep up at the end of the day, and I won't even raise my feet for the broom. I was so stiff, I didn't even lean on the back of the chair. Her pregnancy was great for my posture. West Point would love me.

"I can't touch you."

My fingers withered into a frozen curl when she laid her hand on mine, prying the cardboard, she unbent them. I wondered what wrinkled mess would be left of my hand after she straightened it, what my fingers would look like after she broke their balled-up paper shape. She pulled my hand across the table and put it on her belly.

"Go ahead, it's okay. You can touch me. I'm not contagious. But I have to warn you . . ." (I felt the thing inside rollicking under my fingertips, punching and stabbing, in utero kung fu.) "You are a carrier."

There was a whirling electric current spiraling up my spine, then an awful chugging up from deep in me, were these buried tears? or maybe convulsive twitching that would shake down the sticks of my skeleton? I sat there, with the parasite bounding about under my hand, shocked to hear, mumbling, hesitant, then stuttering till it filled my whole head, laughter pump out my throat.

Okay, okay, here's the deal. She's going to have something we'll simply fling off the ridge into the gully, let the raccoons take it apart. It won't matter a tick. Look at that belly. Too many bags of potato chips. But the diet is brief, a few hours and schlub, splash, the fat slips out. Bundle it up in cotton wadding and you're good as new. The easiest diet you ever had.

Something in the way she held my hand on that thing, I thought, if this is laughter, let me cry.

"Do you want to give it up?"

"I have to."

"Why do you have to?"

"We talked about it. It made sense."

"Do *you* want to give it up?"

She looked at me.

"Do you want to?"

She looked at me.

"Do you?"

She looked at me.

"They're crazy, right? You said they were. We always said they were. Remember, we agreed. When everything flew around us, and the old lady screamed, the walls cracked with the strain of her voice, I'd say, Are they crazy? You'd say, Yes, they're crazy. They're cracked. Not only the walls, but the old lady is, too, cracked as they come. You remember that? Laughing. Don't forget that. Because if you do, I will, too. And then everything will make sense. Her sense. We'll be dead."

"They are crazy. And they said I have to give it up. It's the only way. They're crazy and I believe them."

CHAPTER SIX

BLESS ME, FATHER

BROTHER:

Then it arrived.

By breech.

When they went off to the hospital. I'll tell that later.

They left for the hospital, yelling at each other, crying. The old man left his cigarettes behind, in the middle of the living room floor where they fell.

Spilled out.

I sat on the couch after they left and looked at them. White sticks. Four white sticks spilled out of the pack, lying there. And matches to fire them up. Four spilled out and a fifth part way out of the pack. Waiting to ignite. I sat on the couch and couldn't move my arms or legs. I was knotted. Or clotted. Or clogged rigid. I wasn't allowed to go with them. Too many people. The car too full. Too many of us at the hospital. I wasn't authorized. Only the husband, or in his absence, the parents of the mother. I was one of the neighbors waiting for news, speculating about the outcome, only there were no neighbors, just me. I ate sometime in the night. Something. There were dirty dishes on the couch. I kicked one off when I rolled over in the middle of the night. Broken dreams interrupted by the clatter of the plate. I didn't know how I could have slept when she needed me. But I did. I admit it. I'm ashamed of it. Now four cigarettes, the pack with one part way out, the matches, and the plate on the floor. I didn't remember going to sleep, stretching out on the couch. Shamed.

The telephone didn't make a sound. It was silent as they wanted it. The telephone wasn't going to blab to the neighbors, me.

The pain she huddled over when they walked out.

More later.

Yes, I slept. How could I? I sat on the couch and pounded my thigh with my fist to make up for it. To remind me there is suffering. As though I had forgotten. I thought to shove a knife into myself. But didn't. Coward.

The streetlight bled in the window and I half dreamed shadows striding the room. His chair has grown huge, and breathes. The overstuffed chair stuffed with breathing has grown almost to the ceiling and walks around the room, around the cigarettes, almost stepping on them, almost stepping on them, almost, ohhhhh, almost, watch out, the chair leaning over me and pushing its rough upholstery against my cheek and when it breathes in, I am crushed by its weight, its size, pushing it away takes more strength than I have. It backs away from me, it knocks the lamps, the tables sideways. His chair smells deeper of them than his own hands. Catches oil from his skin, a brown net of breath from his mouth, thick farts, flakes of scalp, crud. The telephone says nothing.

All the waiting in our lives is not as long as this waiting.

"Sign the fucking paper!"

More about that.

I can hear her fingernails clicking and she's not even here.

I can't call anybody. There are no friends to talk to. I can't tell anybody. I won't blab. I won't, never, or you'll never tell me anything, will you? Her nail file is sawing at her nail. She's not here. But she's ever vigilant anyway. She *knows*. I don't whisper into my pillow for fear some hidden microphone will hear. I won't ever whisper. Please fill my mouth with sand. To be sure I'll be silent. Our whole lives take place in this room, this *living* room, and yet, to tear her in half, they took her away.

Dawn, yet the more light floods in, the more blurred my eyes. The deadness at the ends of my arms and legs. Tingling. Bounce a penny on my stomach. It has been hard all night. But not torn in two. It is only hard. Why can't I get sick?

And I don't believe the telephone when it rings. I listen to it, say, What do you want, stupid? You think I believe you're ringing, you're not going to ring ever, are you, and it rings and rings, rattles and yips. I looked at it with my bleeding eyes, rancid breath, palms losing even the pins of feeling that remained, and said, "Hello?" though I couldn't remember even picking it up.

"Get your ass down here and take your mother home. I'm going to stay for a while."

Then I feel how cold the receiver is against my lips and how hard it feels against my temple where I hit it and how quiet it is when I hunch over the kitchen counter and listen to the silence on the phone. I rap the hook a few times to get him back, wondering how the old man got into the room and gone so suddenly.

Another voice, "If you'd like to make a call, please hang up and try again. If you need help, hang up, then dial your operator."

Hello? He was here in the house with me, for a second. I thought he was. I wasn't sure. Now, though, now I knew I was alone in the house.

"If you'd like to make a call, please hang up and try again. If you need help, hang up, then dial your operator."

The next moment in front of the hospital, watching the old lady come down the concrete steps, her face spastic with suppressed tears, then quickly smearing with them. Falling into my arms, a dying ball of rags.

"Oh, God, what she went through. She went through so much."

Everything inside me flutters and jerks.

"How is she?"

"She suffered, horrible. It was breech. Horrible. I couldn't stand her screaming. She was screaming to wake the dead. I never, even with you, never saw so much trouble. Breech is the worst."

"Will she live? Will she walk?"

She bowed her head and I cold feel the back of my throat swelling. I took her by the shoulders and shook her, "Will she live?"

"She'll live. But she suffered. A breech."

What's that mean?"

Breech. I scoured my mind for sense to it. A break. A breach in the wall. Had the walls of her stomach split open? Breach, fissure, fracture, bone fracture? Her bones cracked with the pressure? The armies attacked and breached the walls. Our lives breached. Everything broken.

"It's when the baby comes out feet first. It's supposed to be head-first. The head is smooth, opens everything up so the rest can spurt out. There you go. But when it's feet first, the legs kick everything out of order. The doctor can't get a grip. It tears a woman up, makes her come apart inside. Sixteen hours screaming. I didn't think she could scream anymore. The baby wouldn't come."

Of course it wouldn't. It didn't want to. It held on, dug its tiny fingernails into her slippery organs, used its feet to kick up into her, gripping the ropes of intestines, biting bladders and glands for a hold. Of course it didn't want to come out. It paddled backwards against the push, it clung on for dear life to the inside of her heart, tugged membrane from her chest cavity, trying to wedge its hand between the ribs. Of course it fought the push, that discard, that loathsome bloodsucker, freeloader.

"It had the cord tied around its neck."

It tried to hang itself rather than face us. It knew, it knew what was waiting for it. It looped the umbilicus and throttled its own screams, and then feeling it tighten, got frightened and tried to kick its way back up inside her. A suicide with second thoughts. It pulled on the rope that was attached to her, like raveling of twine, it unsnarled her carefully folded bowels, the slush of release, her screams as her insides untied, flubbed down her, around the baby, like a tub of fish guts, into the hands of the panicked doctor, the hysterical nurses.

"The doctor said she lost a lot of blood."

Teeth and nails tearing her, the plumbing smashed by those peddling limbs, gushes of blood, fountains shooting across her vast inside cavity, brimming in her tubes and channels, overflowing, geysers rising suddenly and falling as quickly, red spits from tiny punctures, arteries severed, flooding, heavy, thick pulsing out of her, pushing the birth table, gored veins splashing her crimson juice.

"And she kept screaming, 'Get this thing out of me. Please, please get it out, please get it out!" We could hear her all the way down the hallway. Your father took a pack of cigarettes out of a nurse's hip pocket and didn't even ask her, took it and smoked it all."

A stream of blood under the operating room door, the nurse rushing out, my sister's blood streaked the shiny floor, from their shoes, running from death in there. The air darkened with smoke as the human smidgepot tried to cover her screams with blindness.

"Your father is going to stay with her. She's sleeping now."

It did this to her, and she spoke for it.

She spoke crazy.

She lugged it around in secret for months, and then tottered around room to room, after it was found out, using chair backs and doorjambs to stay upright. For it. And it does this to her.

"It's a girl. We saw it. Big, nine and a half pounds, and healthy. A beautiful baby. So put your fears to rest, the baby is fine."

Who cares? It did this.

Because she wasn't in labor.

They weren't going to the hospital, that's not what yesterday was about, but when they did leave, the old man was holding one arm and the old lady was holding the other, screaming, "You're going to sign the paper!" and the old man shouted to me, "Get the door, get the door, asshole!" And propped between them, she was shouting, "I can't sign! She won't let me! I want to! She won't let me!" They were gone, to the hospital, the house hushed, the wind-bent house talked to me quietly, the shouting gone, only the house there talking to me.

Because that thing in her knew, it had listened to everything and knew, this was the moment, when they'd beaten her down, and my sister said, "You're right, it's the only way to save ourselves. Let's go." It knew when it heard her say that, and leaped, did somersault twirls inside her, she buckled over, "Mama!"

She put her hands between her legs, her fingers came away soaked. "It hurts, Mama, it hurts!"

"God Almighty!"

"Guy, her water broke!" Grabbing her by the arm, "Don't think this means you're not going to sign, young lady," and turning to the old man saying, "We'll stop on the way."

But it was too late.

They didn't stop at the adoption office. Though EVERYTHING WAS ARRANGED. Though they'd used GOOD JUDGMENT and FORESIGHT. Though PEOPLE WERE WAITING. Though it would ONLY TAKE A MINUTE. Though it was, clearly, the SENSIBLE THING TO DO, they didn't stop.

And she didn't sign before it came. The adoption people had talked to them, to her. They said she had to think about it a week, since the baby wasn't born yet, and then come back and sign. The old lady wanted to know, "Couldn't we take the papers with us?" No, she had to sign in front of the social worker, to make certain she was doing this of her own free will, completely understanding what it meant, though she was planning to sign.

It wouldn't let her sign.

Before she left, she plopped down on the couch and said so, she said, "She doesn't want this."

"Who?"

"Her," pointing to her stomach.

We were in the living room, they all had their coats on.

"What are you talking about? C'mon, let's go."

"I can't go."

"What do you mean, you can't go. You have to. THERE ARE PEOPLE WAITING."

The old man said, "Goddamn it, get your ass up."

Sullenness washed over her face, like someone fed her a spoonful of Crisco. She held that ball in her stomach, clutching it like a football, expecting them to pile on her.

"You should have thought of this before we got half the goddamn city standing by."

The old lady huffed, "This is ridiculous. Is this manners? Keep people waiting. Where do you get these ideas?"

And she said it talked to her through her stomach, she heard it all the time, crazy, crazy talk, and they told her how we'd die if she kept it, did she want that, how it would kill us, and when she finally said, "Okay, let's go," it leaped.

It did this to her.

And the old man leaped and grabbed her and the old lady leaped and grabbed her, and I opened the door like a fool.

There were cigarettes all over the floor.

SISTER:

Having her was the most amazing orgasm I ever had. Oh, my God, it was wonderful.

MOTHER:

Bless me, Father, for I have sinned WHAT ARE YOU DOING HERE? It has been months, a year since my last confession, I'm pretty sure I went at Christmas, I'm not sure I KNOW HOW LONG IT'S BEEN, IN SPIRITUAL TERMS, AN ETERNITY. My God, I am heartily sorry for having offended thee I HAVEN'T MISSED YOU. I WAS HOPING YOU WOULDN'T COME BACK. Since my last confession, it grieves me to tell it, I have committed a mortal sin, Father, and I'm here to beg forgiveness and suffer Thy just punishments DON'T WASTE MY TIME It happened so quickly, at the hospital, the day after the baby was born, it was over before I even knew I was going to do it A LOT OF YOU PEOPLE USE THAT EXCUSE, DON'T YOU? It was her fault, laying there like the Queen of Sheba in that bed, with that thing sucking on her, she didn't even have the decency to wait until we were gone, she rolled back her smock, and in front of us, I don't mind, after all, I'm a woman, but in front of her own father, she should be ashamed, shouldn't she, Father? YOU'RE A DISGUSTING WOMAN There were nurses in and out, and attendants, some of them boys her own age, Father, shouldn't she be ashamed of that? That thing making a sucking noise it was driving me crazy, like those mud fish we saw at Point Pelee when we were standing on the wooden walk among the reeds, black, dirty mud fish, snorting and sucking the filth YOU'VE ALWAYS BEEN A DISGUSTING WOMAN and I still had the thought that I could save my family so I was talking to her about it, telling here that when we left the hospital in a couple of days, we'd simply stop by the place where they sign the papers, and she could leave the baby right there in the hospital, it'd be whooshed away, she'd never have to see it again AND YOU EXPECT FORGIVENESS FOR THAT? We all agreed it would be the best, or we had agreed, before the thing came out of her, it's a pretty baby, but you can't get sentimental when you're trying to save a family, only I didn't realize we didn't agree anymore. She was looking at me and chewing her lip so hard I thought it was going to bleed, and the baby was sucking and my husband had his jaw clenched so I could see that muscle on the side of his jaw stick out and I was talking to her, all our mouths were busy doing something but mine was at least trying to keep everything on track, get something done, be productive, but every time I managed to get a thought lodged in her brain, that thing sucked it out of her, I'd speak, it'd suck, I wasn't getting anywhere MAYBE YOU'LL ALWAYS BE A DISGUSTING WOMAN. And I don't know, God, Who is all good and deserving, You be the judge, can I help it that I get these thoughts stuck in my head, a thing runs round in my brain and I can't get it out until I do something about it like when the kids were little and they'd chew with their mouths open, making all kinds of squishy eating noise, enough to turn my stomach, I certainly couldn't have company over if they were going to eat like that, so I'd tell them to eat with their mouths closed, the boy was the worst, he didn't catch on, he seemed to be completely oblivious even when I reminded him, and then I got to where I would tap him on top of the head with my finger every time he started that awful habit, but let me tell you, Father, I was getting a sore finger, and it wasn't Doing any good, he didn't seem to care, or didn't get it, or maybe boys are slower than girls because I don't remember my daughter having that much trouble learning to eat right, but what's worse, I couldn't stop thinking about it, every little crackle and squish in his mouth got my attention, even ones that a polite eater wouldn't have been able to help make, and I got desperate to make him eat right, I couldn't get the thought out of my head, it would bother me for half an hour after we sat down at the table, dreading that I would have to continue his eating lesson, and he wouldn't catch on, and afterwards, during dishes, it'd take me half an hour to calm down after his eating lesson, so I finally found a way to get his attention and not have to say a word to him, it worked, but you see I couldn't rest until I had it solved, the thought stuck in my head, it went round and round till I was dizzy, what I did, Father, was simply reach over and swat him underneath the jaw when it hung open and he was squishing, his teeth would click, sometimes he bit his tongue, but you know what, Father? He learned fast. YOU FIT THE PHRASE, "FALLEN INTO DARK-

NESS," YOU KNOW THAT? And maybe it was because that baby was slurping and gobbling, I wanted to get it all cleared up, so I was telling her, "You've got to sign the paper, we'll go right over there from the hospital, you *will* sign, you *will*," and I repeated it so often because she had a look like she wasn't hearing what I said, so I wanted to make sure HOW CAN YOU CONFESS WHEN YOU DON'T EVEN KNOW WHAT YOUR SINS ARE? She was pressing that thing closer against her so I grabbed her elbow and started to shake her and said, "You know we don't have the cash for this, you're going to be home, useless, and the bills don't wait, and your brother isn't worth five cents yet, it's all on me because your father is a deadbeat now that he sits around and so you have to sign the paper," and I leaned up close to her and her eyes were clouding up and then I heard behind me, he said in his gruff, no respect for the wife who loves him voice, "Keep the baby. The little shit is ours. We own it." I whirled around and he was looking at me, I've never seen his face so nasty and what does he contribute? What right? And before I knew what I was doing, I clipped him across the face with the back of my hand and, Father, there was a line of blood across his cheek where my engagement ring sliced through the skin, oh, Father, I firmly resolve to sin no more and to avoid the near occasions of sin, with my whole heart and whole soul, and beg the angels of the Lord and the help of His Grace to be made worthy again, she screamed and nurses came running in and everybody in the place knew what happened because he didn't even reach up and wipe away the blood, I was so embarrassed that he let everybody see what he'd made me do YOU'LL HAVE TO SAY AT LEAST TEN THOUSAND "HAIL MARY'S FOR THIS ONE, FIFTEEN THOUSAND "OUR FATHER'S And I haven't felt so alone since I was married, not since I was a little girl and my mother told me how awful I am, and I know I'm awful, but I tried to raise my sisters and brothers right, because she wouldn't lift a finger after she sat down on the wicker chair on the porch, she'd yell, and she'd tell me how I'd never be good enough for her, but how could I be? I was a little girl and I didn't know the first thing about how to raise them, I had to learn and had her yelling at me all the time, so I did everything as perfect as I could, always, I tried not to draw attention to myself, but worked and worked and sewed and cooked and cleaned the house like her slave, it was the only way to keep her off my back, but even that didn't help, she still told me I had bad thoughts, multitudes of evil notions she knew about, and she was right, when I was scrubbing on my knees all the way down the basement steps, one by one, every time I lifted the bucket down a step, I imagined I was putting it down on her face, and no matter how I tried to stop those thoughts, they kept coming, I was ashamed then, too, I've always been ashamed, and I only try to make everything work right and so I depend on merciful God, Giver of pardon and Lover of our salvation to tell me I'll escape the judgment of punishment. YOU MIGHT BE EXPECTING TOO MUCH FROM HIM When all I've ever been trying to do is push and tug and straighten and help, I've had to swat and shove, yes, but it was to make everything work right, and isn't Right what we've needed in this world? Isn't Right what we should all be encouraged to do? My mother held me against the refrigerator and made me put my hands down at my side because I did things wrong, left dirt on the floor, missed a streak, and slapped me silly, and I know it's what a woman can expect, I remember visiting my grandmother and standing outside the screen door on the sidedrive and hearing yelling inside so I went in with my sister and we found my grandfather down on his hands and knees with the razor strop whipping at the end of his arm, lashing my grandmother under the bed, and she said it, too, it's what a woman has to take, and she yelled to us, calmly, from under the bed, "It's okay now, you kids, you go home, go on now, and don't forget to kiss your mother," as the strap painted welts on her thigh, so when my mother hit me, I didn't think it was wrong, I learned to live with it, but none of them seems to have, my family I didn't teach as good, because she said to me, with that thing sucking on her still, right in front of me, of him, of the nurses, "I'm not going to give her away," and I could never do anything like that to my mother, how could she do it to me, wasn't I supposed to do something then, wasn't that my job? To save my family? But I didn't do anything, Father. MAYBE YOU CAN BE FORGIVEN AFTER ALL I knew that baby was beautiful and I couldn't give it away either, and we would take it home, Father, and even if we starve, even if they throw us out in the street, because even if I work twenty four hours a day I can't make enough money to keep us going, I'm afraid I've done something bad, but I don't know what, this sin of letting them keep the baby, Father, is it a mortal sin? This burden I'm letting fall on my family, tell me what to do, Father, tell me the penance, I'll do any penance, Father, I'll wash every pew in the church and shine all the candlesticks, anything, Father, tell me my penance. YOU'VE ALREADY DONE IT, CHILD Free me from the evil desires, sins and temptations of the devil, from the sudden pains of hell YOU'RE GOING TO SUFFER THE PAINS OF HELL, CHILD, UNTIL THE DAY YOU DIE Why, Father, why? IT'S YOUR NATURE God the gracious God the redeemer God the bright God the amiable God the wise God the giver of this perpetual fear wrest me from this agony *NOT IN YOUR LIFETIME, CHILD, NOT WHILE YOU BREATHE ON THIS EARTH* Help me, Father, forgive me for not giving up the baby. Amen.

FATHER:

There are some who try to slip out a fart like it don't belong to them. Shift in their seat, squirm around, looking furtive. A flush starts around their collar and runs like a busting thermometer to the top of their head. They pray we don't guess what they're doing to the upholstery. Step on an elevator sometimes and goddamn, the place stinks like the inside of old Pic*asso*'s asshole, and the guy in the corner is looking up at the floor counter so intent you think his neck is stuck in a crimp.

Every one of us pollutes the atmosphere, every one.

The prettiest woman in slinky silk jammies striding the cliffs of Morocco, you see her there in a perfume ad, smile fixed, hair perfect, body you want to shellack and save for some cold winter night, you can bet her butt cheeks are poofing out with every step. She's thinking, Thank God the wind is coming up fast from the sea because that photographer would fall over dead with the smell. Poof, poof. The President up there at a press conference, bullshit flopping out his mouth? You can bet there's little pops and wheezes out his behind. Right there in front of America. TV cameras whirring, photographers flashing, ten thousand people clambering for his opinion, you can bet somewhere in the back of his head, he's wondering if the secret service man standing at his rear will ever talk to him again. Raquel Welch regrets her burritos as much as the rest of us. A doomsayer preacher points his finger and declares America stinks, it's because he got an inspired thought, it came to him as he was standing there on the podium, suffering a gas leak.

I don't know how, but there's a lot of people forget what they do. They smell to Fare Thee Well one minute and act Holier Than Thou the next. You look at Detroit some sunny morning as you're driving downtown and you'll see a brown tinge over the whole goddamn city. I mean to tell you there's some serious farting going on. Why does everyone deny it?

My philosophy is lift your leg and let her rip.

Admit you stink.

You don't fool anyone anyway.

Call a fart a fart and save us a lot of heartache. I never had a bigger laugh in my life than when my sister farted in Sunday School and I looked at her and she looked at me and I farted and then she farted and then the kid across the aisle farted, and we were all giggling till we couldn't help farting some more and two girls behind me went, "Phew!" and one of them laughed so hard she farted and the room was sounding off rips and fuffs and machine gun sputters and one kid dropped a turd in his pants, and the room stunk like the inside of a Port-A-John on Diarrhea Day in December. I'm telling you it was a goddamn relief after tying our feet in hard sole shoes and pulling on crisp pants and the girls in their Sunday best dresses so they couldn't run around, and having to sit there forcefed God by this lady talked in a wheezy whisper like the words were too hot for her tongue to handle. Boy, we let them rip. She gave my head a good bang on the desk. But it was worth it. We were drowning in the Holy Spirit of Fart.

And not to make too big of claims, but I always thought if Management and the Union would get contract negotiations off with a good fart session, we wouldn't have been out on strike so much. Let's admit who we are and what we are and hold our noses if we have to. The air clears. You don't have to wait long. Stop trying to keep up a lot of unhealthy appearances. Suffering with cramps while we try to get down to the business at hand, whatever it is. You've got to wonder if farting is the root of the troubles between the sexes. Men fart. Woman are always trying to hold them in. No wonder women are so goddamn irritable. They're jealous, for Christ's sake. Women let this goddamn politeness get in the way. We're standing around with embarrassed looks on our faces. When the fact of the matter is, the human body is two-thirds water, one third fart and the rest is a little skin and bone to keep us from leaking apart and blowing away.

Hell, you don't believe me, look in your shorts. Admit there's a stain.

And this all came to me in the hospital when she was shaking the girl's arm, the baby was wobbling against her tit and she called me a deadbeat. I said to myself, tired of holding my breath, tired of holding in something worse than a fart, I said to myself, "Yeah, I'm a deadbeat and that's my granddaughter." And goddamn if it didn't seem like I'd been spending a lot of time denying the stink in my life. And I said, "Who claimed you have to have a job to have a granddaughter?" That much I know I said out loud. She whipped around and slugged me with the back of her hand, and when the nurses ran in and the baby howled and the whole goddamn place turned to pandemonium, I thought, "Ah, shit, it's mine, it's all mine." I didn't cover up the cut on my cheek because I wanted to admit that, too. She looked like she'd explode right in front of me and like when she had her hysterectomy, how it took days after the operation for the gas to get out of her and when it did, it came in long, drawn out, full fledged farts that she wanted to hide in a closet to get away from, but she couldn't help, the first time I ever heard her fart in all these years, but in that embarrassment and shame there was relief, too, and that's what I saw for a second, on her face, when she couldn't run from it anymore and she had to admit that little stinker was ours.

SISTER:

He said, “Stuff a rag in that goddamn brat,” but I knew what he was really thinking.

He said, “I thought I was done scraping mustard out of diapers,” but I knew what he was really thinking.

He said, “Give me some peace, please God, some peace,” but he didn’t fool me. I saw right through him.

Why else does he insist on washing her diapers himself? Why else does he hold my elbow when I go up and down stairs? Why else does he blow funny farts on her belly when he’s done drying her? Why else does he run in there, ahead of me, when she squeaks? Not because he doesn’t have anything better to do, not out of boredom, not fear something is really wrong, not out of disgust because I can’t move fast, until I heal. Not out of habit. Because he hasn’t been around a baby since we were little.

He walks her around on his shoulder, patting her buns, saying, “Hey, you little shitass, can the noise. Sleep. C’mon, close your trap before I give you to the rag man. Yes, I will, I will, too. I’ll roll you in a forty pound brown paper sack and toss you in the incinerator. You trying to ruin my nerves, huh, you little shitass? Like a chainsaw on a violin, you playing my nerves, ain’t that right, you little shitass?” But he holds her like she’s a china teacup so delicate she’ll crumble in his hands, afraid she’ll fall apart like ashes. His hand bumps her rear end gentle, with a soft shushing rhythm on the plastic, and even when she’s caved in with drowsiness, lolling against him, he doesn’t put her down. He paces the length of the house, peers out at the neighbors over the kitchen curtains, rolling foot to foot, patting her, long after she’s drifted away. His voice comes in gentle waves, too. The meanest words he can think of come out in a growling lullaby.

But for me, silence. After he spoke in the hospital and said we’d keep her, he didn’t speak to me again for three days. It almost killed me. He always yells at me. That's how I know I'm in the room. This silence. I'd catch him looking at me when I was holding her. He'd look away. Then he started ordering me around, telling me to cover her head when we went outside. He'd tell me one of her arms was tied up when I was dressing her, he'd say her hair should be pushed back from her ears, and he's reach over and wisp it back. And I couldn't figure what it meant. Does he hate me with a deeper hate than ever before, does he want to take the child and throw me out, will he freeze me to death and take her for his very own? Am I doing everything wrong again? Does he have to correct me to save the girl? I was jelly inside when he spoke to me, thinking I can't be a mother, I don't know how to do this with her.

But then I found out what he was really thinking. And no matter what he says or what he does, I know, and I'm never going to forget it.

Because I paid attention in bed.

You have to pay attention in bed. That's when you find these things out. Everything gets liquid and mingles with everything else, sometimes babies get born, from the mingling. But when I swim through dreams with my eyes open, and lay quiet in the dark, listening, I find out things, real things that aren't covered by the noise of yelling, slamming doors, furious dish washing, angry hammering and sawing. In the night, lying still, when the edges of my skin blur with shadow, I don't know where I begin and where I end, I find things out.

She was sleeping in the crib across from my bed. (Didn't I tell you, sweets, we'd share this room forever?) Lying still, floating in aimless thoughts, I listened to her breathing catch, bubbling, steady beside me, loving her and fearing her because she meant so much, because of what she demanded of me. And thinking mother would come out of the walls and slap me, too, if I rolled over too loud or talked to myself, and the sheets would crisscross with threads of blood, like his cheek. I was still as a pillow, doughy, feeling heavy and fat, when the doorknob turned and the ghosts in the walls jumped, long shadows bent toward me. Trembling, frozen in a headlight, a flashlight, or maybe the hall light, a rapist's dark form blocked the doorway, I sunk into the sheets, blending with them, fearing the Angel of Death, unable to move, eyes near closed, cheek pressed to the linen.

He walked quietly over to the crib and reached down to stroke the chubby hooks balled against her face. And I loved him that he loved her. And then he straightened and turned to my bed, stood over me, towering to the ceiling, and then folding down, seeming to fall forward and turn to cover me, to bury me, swinging around at the last moment to crush the edge of the bed, where he sat next to me.

I didn't breathe.

Or open my eyes.

He lit a cigarette and sat there. The room smelled of smoke and him. He was so still I almost thought he'd gone, but he'd blow smoke out, long drawn out, thoughtful, and then he talked, low, so low I could barely hear him.

"You been a pain in the ass from the time you crawled out from between your mother's legs. I didn't know what to do with you. You weren't happy to be here, I wasn't happy to have you. I thought all you was was whining. A girl, Jesus Christ, how'd I get a girl? If anybody was ill-equipped to raise a girl. But I got one. I got you. I didn't want to hurt you, but I didn't want to have anything to do with you either. I guess God (if there is one) would forgive me for being confused. But that didn't help you any, did it? And I didn't know why you always had to piss and moan, and at the time all I wanted was peace and quiet. Maybe that's the time you *had* to piss and moan, had to have something from me I didn't want to give. Well, you didn't get it, did you, girl? That was my fault. I did all the right things, without doing the right thing. Which was be there for you. I always thought you were pissing and moaning because that's what you were, a pisser and a moaner. I don't have any use for that. I was wrong, wasn't I? You were standing up to me, weren't you? In the only way you knew how. You were saying, 'Hey, old man, look at me,' weren't you? And I kept my hand over my eyes like I was ashamed of you. I found that out at the hospital. When you stood up to both of us, and you said, 'Look at me and look at my baby and fuck you, old man, and fuck you, old lady: I demand.' I don't know how I got it stuck in my head that you weren't good for anything. You got some nerve. You showed me you got some nerve, and now I know there's more to you than I ever guessed."

He sat there through another cigarette, and when he put it

out, he reached over and ran his fingers through my hair, and I felt stirring, I wanted to give him something, I wanted him to have something I didn't know what, something important, I wanted to give him my baby, I loved him that much, and then he was gone, clicking the door shut soft behind him.

MOTHER:

"You're going to ruin that child."

"I have to encourage her, don't I?"

"Well, of course you've got to encourage her. I've always said you have to encourage children."

"Well, mother, that's what I'm doing."

"You don't encourage her by running in there every time she makes a peep. You're only encouraging her to peep a lot."

"Well, how do you suggest I encourage her."

"Teach her who's boss."

"You think she'll find that encouraging? Teaching her she works for me when she's still in the crib?"

"I didn't say she *works* for you. Don't be stupid."

"Well, isn't that what a boss is?"

"I meant if you don't teach a child to adhere to your schedule, she'll run you ragged."

"I don't mind."

"Well, it'll ruin her."

"How?"

"She'll think all she has to do is squawk and the whole world will come running."

"Well, that's true. I'm her whole world and I'll come running. Shouldn't I teach her the truth?"

"I think you don't want to learn anything about how to raise a child. You know everything. Well, I've been through it twice already so don't tell me."

"Yeah, and look at us."

"What?"

"Nothing."

"You'd think you would pay attention. When I say encourage a child, I don't mean giving in to her every whim."

"What whims? Food, a dry diaper and to be held and talked

to. Mother, those are hardly whims."

"Well, nobody on this earth gets what they want any time they want it. I made sure you kids knew that from the time you were crawling on your knees. You have to wait for things. You have to pay attention to other people's needs. And I think you should make an effort not to spoil her. You're taking the easy way out again. Because it's easier to run in there and shut her up than it is to exercise a little self-discipline and let her cry. So she learns self-discipline. Your problem is you don't have any self-discipline yourself."

"You let me cry when I was a baby?"

"Not all the time. But enough so you knew you couldn't run me ragged."

"Well, you see how much self-discipline I got out of it."

There she went, twisting my words again. Honestly, if I didn't know better I'd say they were ganging up on me. He's as bad as she is. You'd think he'd understand at least. When I pointed out she runs in there any old time that baby makes a sound, he shrugged his shoulders and said, "Why the hell not?" Now how are we supposed to have a conversation if that's the way he's going to talk?

Why the hell not? I'll tell you. Because it's not right, that's why. There's the slightest yip or burble from that back room and the two of them chase in there like the roof's falling in. It's not right. Nobody comes running when I make a sound. I could scream bloody murder and they'd stand over that crib without flicking a glance in my direction. And I'm the mother around here. You're at least supposed to notice the mother, aren't you?

Even the things I could help her out with, that I'm unquestionably trained to do better than her, she interferes. Won't take advice. Won't take the most obvious help. She finally sat the child down to trim her hair. About time, too. No telling what was growing in it. It may be fine hair, but there are a lot of things you can't see with the naked eye that could be clinging to the strands. Especially in a baby's hair, you never know. They play with their feces one minute and their face the next. That's why you keep it short. Or at least that's what a mother who knows what she's doing would do. A responsible mother. She waved the scissors around the child's head, she might as well have been trying to fan it dry for all the hair she was taking off. I couldn't stand to see her floundering around with a chore I can do for her professionally, so I reached for the scissors and said, "Here, let me do that."

She snapped them away from me and said, "I'll give the haircuts to my daughter." I thought she was going to spit in my eye. Where do these snits come from? You try to help.

Even he could do a better job than she was doing.

I don't know where things are going around here.

It makes me tired. I'm tired all the time, in fact, I'm exhausted. Work all day, and then come home and everybody ignores you. I don't know. I feel like somebody's grandmother or something. And that's another thing. He can stop calling me, "Grandma." And so can she. She looks up from the crib when I come in the room and says, "Look, honey, Grandma's here." It always makes me look behind to see what old lady she's talking about.

Well, I am a grandmother, I admit, but she doesn't have to say it so everybody in the world hears. Let other people figure it out for themselves. Why can't I simply be nice to the baby like I'm her mother, why do I have to be the grandmother? I'll have to bake cookies all the time, and God, on top of having to work every day. Will it never end?

Then with an all-knowing smile, the witch next door stopped me on the sidedrive and said, "I see you have a new addition to the family." Oh, she's so smart. Everybody is so damn smart these days.

I felt like she kicked me in the stomach. I wanted to fall down on the cement and curl up with my hands over my head to protect myself. I wanted to say, "Where'd you get that idea? There's nothing new over at my house, same old same old. Day after day, you know, same old. Yep, routine. Like clockwork." And I almost did, except that damn smile and the way her brows arched up like it was all so damn funny. She knew. And if she knew so did everybody else. She'd make sure of that. She'd heard the crying. She'd seen us bundle the baby off to the doctor for check-ups. And the part of my stomach that was already hurting, twisted tight, I wanted to say, "You rotten wicked awful woman, you've got no business snooping around my house. Stick your nose up your fanny, what goes on over here is none of your business. You should be ashamed. Snooping. I don't want to see you look at my gutters, you mean beer sopping old slut," words rattling around in me so strong it scared me. I could have scratched out her eyes. I don't want anybody thinking awful things about me, but there she was, ugly, ugly thought all over her filthy puffy bar stool face.

And it happened again. I did it without even thinking, like in the hospital. These things happen. I don't seem to have the slightest control over myself anymore. I do things that surprise me as I do them. I took two steps toward her so fast she rocked back on her heels and almost fell over the bushel basket. I guess I moved so suddenly she was afraid she was going to get it right in the mouth. And like I was watching myself from another planet, like I was some strange creature far away staring down, I saw myself reach into my purse and pull out a whole handful of snapshots we got back from the drugstore, and shove them in her face.

"Oh, you should see her. She's gorgeous. Look at this. When we brought her home. Guy had a fit because she wasn't wrapped up enough. As if he knows anything. And in the bath. Look at that face."

"Uh, your daughter must be getting married pretty soon, or, uh . . ."

Wicked, wicked woman.

"Oh, she got rid of him. A bum. She thought we'd do a better job raising her. And she's right. Look at this. She's a smart one. She hits her dangly toy already. Nobody had to tell her anything. She caught right on."

I could have kicked myself. I wanted to stop and bat that witch in the face. But I kept on talking.

I was behaving like a strange creature.

Like a grandmother.

Father:

I don't mind looking at them, but I never wanted to touch them, peek down their blouses, up their skirts, talk to them, listen to them, pamper them, primp them, push away the hands that stray to the front of my pants. I never wanted a circus of female flesh. Maybe when I was young that's what I wanted, change women as easy as changing my shorts. But not anymore. Now I can grab them and twist them around any way I want. They giggle and fawn. I'm sick from too much sweets. I go home at night I don't even want to see them in a magazine. I'm sick and tired of their flouncing and chatter. The prettier they are, the more inanities come bubbling out of them. You'd think when I rap their fingers with my clippers, they'd get the hint. I cracked a lady the other day so hard her knuckles swelled up. She came in the next week, yanked the shirt out of my waist, and slid a hand all the way up to my hairy nipples.

"I wonder what it's like to fuck a gorilla."

"I wouldn't know," I said, "I never climbed in a cage with one."

She's not thirty years old. What's she want with me?

It's disgusting.

But when she said, "You want the kid, figure out how to pay for it," I had to do something. And this is it.

Honest to God, I tried everything. I stood on Eight Mile and Gratiot with bums so some son of a bitch would pay me two bucks an hour to fling circulars on porches. I worked down at the hardware store with my uncle, who whimpered about church all day, and I got paid worse. I got cramps from scribbling applications, and a blister on my butt from sitting on bus benches, running around the city to apply. I'm no prima donna. I hung around warehouses looking for work. But they thought I was trying to make a score and gave me the bum's rush. There's a guy willing to hire me to sell balloons on lunch hour downtown, but when I was giving change, the goddamn things slipped out of my hand, and I watched that job sail away. The coroner wanted somebody to pick up bodies at hospitals and cart them in. I could have the job, but I needed a station wagon. House painter, bricklayer, lawn cutter, street sweeper, electrician's helper, cab driver, I applied for everything, I'd do anything. I got nothing. Or if I did, they'd tell me they didn't need me the next day or next week. Something. I had my back against a harder, higher wall than it's ever been.

So there was nothing for it but to get some schooling.

I wanted to go to truck driver school, but that cost two thousand dollars.

Electrician, two years, plus union dues.

Anything where you sit down on the job wanted a diploma.

I was desperate, yeah, I'd do anything, but this? I followed the only avenue left for me.

If I wasn't such an asshole when I was seventeen years old, I'd have let the war wait and finished high school. Now I had to go back and pick up the pieces. It was hard begging money from the guys I used to work with, fifty here, sixty there, Davidson, the first I went to, was the worst.

"What do you need this for?"

"I got bills. You can help me out, fine, if not, forget it, it's nothing, don't worry about it."

"You need more? What kinda bills you talking about?"

"I'm going back for job training."

"Good for you. What in?"

No sense hiding. Still it almost killed me the first time I said it out loud. I was doing it, but I hadn't even told her what I was about. But she'd find out. And he might as well know, too. "I'm going to beauty school."

He went slack-jawed, guffawed.

"That's right," I said, and looked him in the eye.

"You son of a bitch, you'll be in Pussy Paradise! You gone, uh, you know . . ." and he crooked a pinkie in the air.

"Bend over that bench. If I get it up, you'll be the first to know."

Son of a bitch called me a couple weeks later and had me come down at lunch. They took up a collection and presented me with most of the tuition, tube of lipstick and pair of lace panties.

In the school we cut hair and made some tips, but it's not until I got in a shop I discovered my real talent for the job wasn't cutting hair, but customer satisfaction. They'd say be nice to the customer, customer's always right, kiss the customer's twat, be a lap dog, give them what they want. So I cut hair and kept my mouth shut. A real effort, these broads tooting off about husbands and kids, their car wasn't big enough, their brat had acne, they don't get laid, trying to resurrect themselves with a haircut. I'd spray them full of frills and fluffs so they could warble at each other when they walked out the door, but I wasn't making much money at it. I ran myself ragged trying to please them: They want it this way, okay, they got it this way, they want it like that, okay, they got it like that. They'd bring in magazine photos and say make me look like her. But you can't make a silk purse out of a sow's ear, and I couldn't even work with the whole ear. All I had was a tuft of the sow's hair. Nothing was good enough for the biddies. There I was wearing an apron, gritting my teeth in a cloud of hair spray. They'd whine to the owner about how their hair didn't "sing," that's what one lady said, her hair didn't "sing." It was piled high, glued stiff, she wanted singing, she should have caged a canary in it. I kept my mouth shut and went back to the task, tried to make it "sing," and had the owner going behind me with her scissors to tuck and clip what I'd done. All I was getting was fat, featherless hens, collapsed, bitchy at the scrambled mess their face and bodies had fallen to. I'd tease the dyed, damaged fuzz on their skulls into curls that didn't do a lot to raise them from the dead.

"Guy, I don't know if you have the touch."

The customers were satisfied, but they weren't singing when they went out the door. My tuition was looking misspent. She didn't know if I had, as she said, a "gift for hair." I considered laying down the comb and going back to my chair at home. Until the day I got this bitch so mean they could have given her two hysterectomies, it wouldn't have improved her disposition.

I was working along and she was critiquing every snip, using the mirror in front of her. Turned away from the mirror, she was still clairvoyant, knew I was fucking up. I picked up the razor, thought to trim a little around her ears and maybe slit her throat, but before I even got it off the counter, she was telling me first I needed to scissor her bangs. Keeping my mouth shut has never been my strong suit, but in beauty work I'd done a better job of it than I ever had. When she started for the eleventh time, I put down the razor and said, "Look, you and me got a fucking problem here." Loud. The whole shop stopped dead. The owner looked up from the till. The other cutters froze over their cuts. The ladies under the driers pushed back the lids.

"You're making a mess. If I don't say something I don't know what I'll have left."

"Shut up. You couldn't comb the hair on my asshole. Who do you think you are?"

The owner was vaulting the counter, but it's a long way from the front of the shop to the back where we were having our little "confrontation."

"You're a bitch because your old man don't put out, am I right? Huh? And he don't put out because you look like a hen's ass. Well, this time you're going to get the cut you deserve."

Fear gripped her face, that is, fear lent a little stiffness to the saggy pouches, like meringue on a lemon pie; her rheumy eyes widened. I pushed her back in the seat.

"You want to make his pecker stand up, I'll show you how."

I started to cut, comb, glue and paste while the old lady turned purple, gagging on her tongue.

The owner sprinted up.

"I'm so sorry, Mrs. Cosima, I'll take over for . . ."

I stuck my razor in her face and said, "Edith, unless you want to lose your upper lip along with your mustache, you go back where you came from."

A head of hair never got cut so fast, or so good. Not that the old lady could see it, simpering in the chair, and the rest of the place was silent.

"You open your mouth like you know what's good for you, you got some notion stuck in your head, stuck like a nail. You make everybody's life hell."

When I put the hand mirror in front of her, she squinted into the glass and pulled a piece away from her temple, about to tell me it should be shorter or longer or curlier or straighter, and I said, "He don't get a hard on tonight, you get your money back tomorrow. Now get out of here."

She left a ten dollar tip.

And she didn't come back. But she did call for an appointment next month.

I walked up to the next lady and motioned her to get up.

Quiet, having seen the whole deal, she whispers, "I think what I want you to do is . . ."

I said, "I don't give a shit what you want."

That's when I started to make some cash. My customers got younger and prettier and richer, and they followed me shop to shop as I moved to better neighborhoods. I developed a "firm style" and the cuts got better and the customers left singing. Then, like I said, they started throwing themselves at me. I thought, Isn't there another working dick in this town? This all they got to do with themselves when I lean over the chair, stick their manicure in a man's business? And as if that's not enough, she started coming home from work with that glint in her eye. Was it because I smelled of perfume? Because my hands were soft? Rewarding me for my job? Or because she knows what goes on in a beauty shop? I don't know. But she wouldn't keep her hands off me. I was afraid to close the bedroom door. I was on my feet all day, I'd try to remind her that we had WORK in the morning, but she kept coming at me. Embarrassment of riches don't begin to say it. Old Henry was gasping for air. I told her to take a Vic Tanny course to work off some of the excess, but she laughed in my face and kept right on coming.